WINDOWS
ON THE SEA

AND OTHER STORIES

WINDOWS
ON THE SEA

AND OTHER STORIES

BY
LINDA SILLITOE

Signature Books
Salt Lake City
1989

For Robert Earl and Phyllis Liddle Buhler—
Lifegivers and Storytellers

© 1989 by Signature Books, Inc.
Signature Books is a registered trademark of Signature Books, Inc.
All rights reserved
Printed in the United States of America

95 94 93 92 91 90 89   6 5 4 3 2 1

Cover design: Traci O'Very

Cover illustration: *Sea Window ,*
Marilyn Miller, serigraph, 1989

Library of Congress Cataloging-in-Publication Data

Sillitoe, Linda, 1948–
    Windows on the sea and other stories / Linda Sillitoe.
        p.   cm.
    ISBN 0–941214–82–6
    I. Title.
    PS3569.I447W56   1989
813′.54—dc20   89–32695
                                                                        CIP

CONTENTS

A STRING OF

INTERSECTIONS

B ECAUSE SHE KNEW SHE LOOKED HER BEST, HER PINK silk blouse ruffling over the lapels of her pink suit, Leah had nothing to do waiting for Karen but to reread the menu. She had arrived at the restaurant early and, after a quick glance through the sparsely populated dining room, ducked into the women's room to smooth her thick blond hair. She hadn't seen Karen, her college roommate, for almost two years, even though they lived in the same city. They talked occasionally on the telephone and always promised to get together soon.

Their husbands weren't particularly compatible, Leah mused, studying the ice water the waiter set before her. That was part of the reason they saw each other so infrequently after being such close friends for years. Not that the men didn't get along. The Skipper, as Leah's husband was dubbed at age four on his father's rented yacht, was adroit in any social situation, and Stuart, Karen's husband, could be intense or, more often, droll. When they got going, Skip and Stu could keep the table lively and had done just that when they were newly married couples. Leah kept a mental photograph of the four of them,

Skip blond and lithe beside her and Stu's and Karen's dark heads across the table, all of them teasing and laughing.

Really, Leah decided, Karen and Stu were probably the best conversationalists she knew. How she had envied Karen in their college days as she watched the two of them locked in discussion for hours on end, never running short of ideas, never finishing their mutual exploration. She and Skip talked the way they made love, for pleasure and purpose, only a means to an end.

Now Skip never suggested dinner with Stu and Karen, Leah thought regretfully. He preferred skyline restaurants with gourmet chefs, where he could court his business contacts. He wanted Leah there in black velvet and diamonds (not that she minded, though she did think the conversations often dull). Stu and Karen were more likely to suggest a barbecue with their children — how old would they be now? — and Bettina, Skip and Leah's toddler. Then the talk ranged from child-rearing to politics, from religious philosophy to movies to books. Skip always seemed to have a good time, Leah thought frowning slightly, then brightening as she saw Karen hurry down the carpeted stairs.

For a second Leah felt ridiculously over-dressed, for Karen wore a classy but not-new sweater over a gathered, paisley skirt and only medium heels. She pushed the feeling away. She was appropriately attired for her job just as Karen, perhaps, was for hers. She half stood and reached for her friend; Karen hugged her, carefully, as if afraid to muss her. "Don't you look gorgeous," she said.

"Here, slide in, it's wonderful to see you. Why has it been so long?" Leah demanded.

Karen laughed and picked up a menu. "Silly, isn't it? We have a lot of catching up to do. I hope you wrote up an agenda."

As Karen studied the menu, Leah covertly studied her friend. That wonderful dark hair still shone and swung, and the hazel eyes were as confidence-inviting as ever. She was still

Karen, all right. But dark shadows under the friendly eyes caught Leah's attention. Lack of sleep? Not really — these purplish stains looked bone deep. And her hands, Leah noticed, weren't cared for — but Karen had always considered nail polish something of a bother.

Karen looked up, saw Leah watching, and Leah thought her eyes grew guarded as she smiled and folded the menu. "Let's order before we start talking," Leah suggested, snapping her elegant fingers for the waiter, who wheeled and approached them at once.

"I'm impressed," Karen murmured, but Leah let it pass. "The artichoke salad, please," she said briskly, "and a glass of Perrier."

"That sounds good," Karen said uncertainly, then added firmly, "I'll have the quiche lorraine and a Coke."

By the time their meals arrived, they had shown photographs of their children, Karen's solemn Anne in her round glasses, the twins beaming, gap-toothed, from their first-grade school pictures, and Bettina chortling merrily in the studio's white wicker chair.

"So she's in pre-school?" Karen asked. "But she's not three yet, is she?"

"Next month," Leah said. "This program combines child care and pre-school so the children really start the activities whenever they're ready. What is it you're doing, exactly?"

"I'm developing a gifted program for middle schools in the district," Karen explained. "I try to actually work with the kids once a month so I can keep in touch with those bright minds. The kids are amazing. I wish all the teachers were!"

"So it's a fun job?" Leah asked, smiling at Karen's evident enthusiasm.

"Very. And what exactly do you do now?"

"Oh, we're both still in the department store. Skip's a department head, but he buys the jewelry and oversees the other lines. I'm what they call a customer consultant. I plan and arrange seminars and fashion shows and consult with our pricier clients."

"Do you enjoy it?"

"I really do, especially the fashion shows." She rolled her blue eyes. "Naturally the models depress me — all those skinny twenty-year-olds prancing around on five-inch heels."

"Why should you care?" Karen assured her. "You look wonderful, perfect." And now I understand why, she thought to herself. It's her job — all day focused on fashion.

"But so do you," Leah protested.

"I have my own system of dress," Karen confided, "called the whatever's-clean-in-the-closet rotation."

They both laughed and for a second it seemed like old times. Maybe Leah hasn't really changed, Karen thought, crazy Leah who stacked dates because she couldn't turn anyone down, who once sneaked a runaway girl into the dorm four consecutive nights one cold December. When the hard-eyed teenager was caught, inevitably, stealing sweet rolls from a 7-11 store, Leah went to the hearing and bawled out a juvenile judge. Karen had half expected Leah to marry someone like Jerry, the handsome stutterer who smiled her through many dates, or Bernard, bright and funny but overweight. All the boys adored Leah in college, it seemed to Karen. What impressed her was that Leah blessed them all, the handsome and homely, the intelligent and dull, with her attention. But she had married Skip, fraternity president, fast-track salesman, now a department store executive, who once had seemed to Karen the most desirable man on campus.

Karen was dating Stuart even then, an intense, interesting, very busy law student with a satirical passion for local politics. Although she and Stu became close friends, Karen couldn't help envying Leah. Skip was so handsome, so suave, and she was sure that his eyes met hers with a particular gleam. Then one night after a movie as the four finished off a pizza, Skip com-

mented meanly to Karen about something she said or wore. Together she and Leah walked back to the car, letting the men go
ahead. "He didn't mean it that way," Leah said anxiously, and
Karen had shrugged, still stung. She could no longer remember
what Skip had said, only her swift gratitude as she climbed in
the back seat with Stu, who folded her in. From that moment
on, she gladly left Skip to Leah.

So now Leah has it all, Karen thought, watching her friend
sort through her salad—money, husband, baby, clothes, success.
Her own life was such a demanding muddle of people and ideas
and talk and emotions. She fantasized about a lonely cabin in a
desert or on a mountain, without a single word in it—no books,
no radio or television, no typewriter or computer. Maybe a camera or a sketch pad, though she was no good at drawing. Maybe
just time and silence. Sleep. Maybe a lover? A mute lover.

"So how's Stu?" Leah was asking. "As I mentioned on the
phone, I bumped into him downtown the other day. I was so
glad to see him!"

"Oh, fine," she said. "He was glad to see you, too."

Leah gave her a searching look. So she wasn't lost under
the polish and pink silk, Karen thought. "Is he better now?" Leah
was asking. "He looks just fine, but I know you were terribly
worried about him when he had the breakdown."

Karen sighed, trying to think how to be brief but honest.
"I'm still worried, although he's certainly better than he was two
years ago. I guess I'm just getting tired of it." She drained her
Coke. "Leah, does he really look fine?" she asked abruptly.
"Doesn't he look older to you—those sad lines in his face?"

Everything's changed, Karen wanted to blurt, but didn't:
the texture of his skin, those nervous little fidgets, the hangdog
look in his eyes, the tentative way he touches me. Everything's
different.

"Oh, we're all older," Leah shrugged. "No, basically he
seemed like the same old funny Stuart."

"Mmmm, good." Karen smiled and said nothing for a minute, trying to make her voice light. "Well, he still has the humorous cadence but some time ago I quit laughing. He just has everyone so well trained to laugh—it's automatic. Once in a while now, he makes me laugh. And then I think maybe he's becoming himself again."

Leah leaned forward across the table. "So it's really been hard. But I thought he responded to the medicine so quickly—really bounced back."

"He did at first. But we've found out there's a lot more to chemical depression than a few pills. The last couple of years have been a real roller coaster ride for both of us."

Leah set her fork delicately on her salad plate and wiped her fingertips on the white linen napkin. "I'm sure you've been a tremendous help to him, Karen. You two have always been so close."

Karen nodded. "Maybe that intimacy has saved us—do you know what the divorce rate is for people with depression?—but it's also been awful. We've depended on each other too much all these years. Stu's my best friend, my lover, my husband. When he caves in or manipulates me or demands tons more than anyone can give, I have to deal with it. Worse, I don't have him for consolation." Her voice broke and she poured some more ice water, biting back tears. When she finally looked up, Leah smiled at her reassuringly.

"Don't give up, Karen. You two have so much going for you, more than any couple I've ever known. And cute children, too."

Karen wrinkled her nose in the old way. "Yeah, it's great being everyone's ideal couple when your marriage crumbles. Listen, don't worry about it. Stu really is doing better—lots better, and the kids are settling down, too. I just have a mild case of battle fatigue. I so seldom talk about this that when I do too much bubbles out. Toads and snakes all over the tablecloth, just like the princess in that awful fairy tale."

"Don't be silly," Leah said. "I'm glad you told me and I'm sure everything's going to be all right. I feel badly that this has been so hard for you, but I have to admit I'd like to have a little more of that intimacy. You know how Skip is—he never really opens up, even to me. He always has everything handled."

Karen laughed. "I'd like to see some of Skip's confidence in Stu again. For so long, his opinion of himself has been below rock bottom."

"Really?" Leah asked, surprised. "Well, you sure can't say that of the Skipper," she drawled, covering up, and they both laughed. "Sometimes I wonder if there isn't a little insecurity somewhere under all that brashness."

"There must be," Karen said. "Didn't you tell me he had a pretty traumatic childhood?"

"Very. Worse than mine, which only contained a divorce. Neither of us talk about the bad stuff. I hate surprises and he wears his armor night and day."

"*We* talk too much," Karen sighed, "but sometimes the talking's still good. We don't know how not to talk, in any case. The kids hate it, but then, they're talkers, too."

"I remember," Leah smiled. "Let's go to lunch again soon, okay?"

"Right," Karen said, reaching for the tab, but Leah already had it.

"I asked this time; your turn next time," she said, extracting a credit card from her tortoise shell wallet.

Back in her cream-colored office, Leah couldn't account for her restlessness. Her afternoon appointment with Mrs. Chandler had been cancelled, and Dee Derringer, supervising next week's fashion show, was unavailable. She felt ruffled, somehow, by her lunch with Karen, but she couldn't place or define her discomfort, which must, she decided, be sympathetic. She suspected that Stu and Karen had been struggling financially during Stu's trouble, for his law practice was modest and teachers didn't make much. Not that she and Skip didn't run short of cash. But Skip had a way of managing when she grew anxious about their debts.

Finally Leah opened her bottom drawer and removed the bottle of pale pink nail polish. She added a fresh coat that was definitely unneeded since she had applied one just before lunch. The telephone rang while she was still waving her left hand to dry it. She startled, picking up the receiver carefully with her right hand.

"Mrs. Vaughn Sheffield?"

"Yes, this is Leah Sheffield." Hardly anyone called Skip by his given name.

"This is Detective Joe Gale."

"Yes?" Detective, did he say?

"Mrs. Sheffield I'm meeting with your husband this afternoon and since some of our discussion will concern you, I'd like you to be present if you can be."

"Oh? Well, what's this all about? Is it the robbery in the jewelry department last month?"

A pause. "That's part of it. Mr. Sheffield said he preferred to meet at your home rather than in the office. I'm on my way there now. Can you join us?"

"Yes, I suppose I can. I'll just be a few minutes. Can't you tell me —"

"Thank you. I'll see you soon."

Leah replaced the receiver and unconsciously checked her left nails to see if they were dry. Why would the detective need to speak with her about a theft in Skip's department? She didn't know anything about it. As usual, she and Skip had driven to work separately; he often needed his car during the day and sometimes she did. She dialed Skip's extension quickly, but Nora, his secretary, said he'd left. She didn't suppose he would pick up Bettina and the detective hadn't said how long this would take. Leah dialed the pre-school and asked if Bettina could stay until six or seven.

The distance from downtown to their condominium just outside the city limits seemed oddly lengthened as Leah drove through the lagging afternoon traffic that had not yet thickened with rush hour. Semaphores turned yellow as she approached. Twice she stopped and the third time went through, narrowly missing a left- turner. A large brown leaf caught under the windshield wiper on the driver's side and flopped hopelessly until she turned on the wipers and let it escape. Why hadn't Skip told her about this meeting? Even a note before he left the office would have helped if he couldn't reach her personally. And why didn't he just have this detective come to his office on the department store's lush executive floor?

He knew that she hated surprises and yet so often he sprang them on her, saying sweetly, "I didn't think you'd mind," or "I called but you were busy," or even "You know I mentioned this last week." Crossly she braked for the red light in the left-turn lane opposite the condominium, trying to assure herself this interview was nothing, would soon be over, and she could punish Skip by making him take her out for lobster.

She closed their front door and walked toward the men, backlit by the western window. One rose, not Skip, and she felt her heart drop.

"Mrs. Sheffield?"

She walked forward and shook hands with the detective, looking past him at Skip, who quirked his mouth at her but said nothing. She sat down on the white couch beside Skip, reaching for his hand, which communicated nothing. The detective, seated in a chair on her other side, gazed at her with intent green eyes. His clothes, she noticed, were rather worn and inexpensive. His right thumb had an ink stain at the knuckle.

"Mrs. Sheffield," the detective began, "for several months I've been investigating some heavy losses at the department store where you and your husband work. You mentioned last month's robbery and, as I said, that's part of my concern, but only a small part. There have been a number of irregularities."

Leah felt Skip's hand jerk. She looked at him, and he withdrew his hand, flashing her a warning look. But what was she doing wrong? She folded her hands in her lap. "What do you mean?"

The detective reached into an old briefcase by his chair and took out a box, which he opened. "Do you recognize these, Mrs. Sheffield?"

Leah took the box and looked carefully. "These are mine!" she gasped. "You found them."

"You recognize these diamond earrings?"

"Yes. Skip gave them to me for Christmas two years ago, and they were stolen about six months later."

"Did you collect insurance for that loss?"

"Yes, of course." He was nodding. She looked at Skip, whose face turned sullen, reviving a flash of deja vu. He looked exactly as he had the day he walked into their laundry room and found her staring at a motel key in her palm. "This was in your pocket," she told him.

"Shit!" he'd said. "Wayne Dewsnup forgot to return that and gave it to me on the way to the airport. I told him I'd drop it off, and it slipped my mind."

He had taken the key and dropped it in the wastebasket. "The motel's probably changed the locks by now, anyway," he said.

Leah had practically forgotten the incident, but the memory of the odd way he'd yanked the key out of her hand and walked stiffly to the wastebasket made her wonder. Now she looked back at the earrings in the detective's hand. They were stunning, the best gift Skip had ever given her.

"So what's the problem?" she asked, not caring that she sounded a little defensive.

"The problem, Mrs. Sheffield, is that your husband sold these earrings to a private client after you collected the insurance money for the theft."

"What?" Leah heard him, but his words didn't register. Her mind seemed to be working in slow motion the way it had the day Bettina fell off a chair and bit all the way through her lower lip, drenching herself almost immediately in blood.

The detective repeated what he'd said, giving her time. She turned to Skip. "Well, that's impossible. I'm sure Skip can explain this . . . "

She waited until he met her eyes. "You sold my earrings?" Her voice squeaked.

Skip shrugged and looked away. "They want a scapegoat, Leah. Hell, can't you see that's what this is about? I've been investigating some problems in the department and someone — probably the guilty party — is setting me up for a fall. Rather successfully, too," he added bitterly.

"How do you know he sold my earrings?" she asked the detective.

"We have the receipt and the buyer is prepared to testify." She looked back at Skip, who was smiling derisively.

"You see, Mrs. Sheffield, we find that certain customers — including some of your creditors — are able to purchase jewelry at a substantial discount from your husband. Also, certain items have disappeared outright and been written off as losses from internal or external theft. We're talking about criminal theft and fraud."

Leah closed her eyes, then opened them and looked from one man to the other. The detective seemed to be making up his mind about something. Skip's face was angry and impassive except for a muscle that jumped in his jaw, as it always did under stress.

"Detective Gale," he said smoothly, "I agreed to speak with you voluntarily without benefit of an attorney. You're completely on the wrong track with these ridiculous accusations, and I think you've outstayed your welcome."

The detective merely nodded and replaced the earrings in his briefcase. Why, Leah wondered, were Skip's steps so jerky as he went to yank open the door? And why did she suddenly want to leave with Joe — wasn't that his name? — who had found the beautiful earrings Skip gave her with a kiss one Christmas morning?

When Karen returned to her office after lunch, she found so many telephone messages that she stayed busy the rest of the afternoon returning calls, leaving the grant writing she dreaded until morning. By the time she left work, the raw edges left by her lunch with Leah were smoothed. How many times had she vowed never to discuss Stu's illness with anyone? No one could understand how someone as bright, as insightful, as sensitive as Stu could become so insecure, so incapable, so needy. She could never articulate her nightmare without sounding and feeling disloyal. Besides, he was much better now. If only they were not both still pursued by the furies of possibility — recalling unwanted the days when he lay grief-racked and helpless for no apparent reason, the nights when he believed he was terminally ill. If now they could forget, if ever the pills and therapy disappeared from their lives, maybe he would truly be well.

Blue shone through the clouds, she noted with approval walking to her car on the top floor of the parking plaza, and the sun's low rays lit the trees like torches. She drove home with the chilly air nipping her cheeks through the open window, late-1960s' songs unwinding from the radio. Not so long ago, she and Stu had sung along, driving from library to hamburger joint, even while studying together for exams. As far as she could see down Thirteenth East, a string of semaphores shone green, and her spirits lifted. She soared through one intersection and timed her speed for the next.

Their house sat at the far end of a cul de sac so that as soon as she approached she could see its yellow windows, glowing like the cottages she had drawn as a child. Stu's car was in the driveway, and both cats crouched on the front window sill, soaking in the leaking heat but unwilling to abandon the crisp autumn night. They would accompany her in, she knew.

Karen fought down her familiar dread, approaching the house — wondering how Stu would be and how his mood might have affected the children. For the moment, she would believe that all was well — and, if not, that she could make it well. She parked behind Stu's car, turned off the key, and swung out of the car, leaves crunching under her shoes. She shuffled them, walking to the porch. Danny and Eric had left a pile of them on the far side of the yard. Maybe she could interest them in a garbage bag.

Beyond the living room, Karen could see Anne perched on the dishwasher in the kitchen, legs crossed, a *World Book* volume on her lap. "Hi, snookums," Karen said, dropping a kiss on the brown head. "What's new?"

"Aphids," Anne said. "I wanted to show dad something." A good sign. When Stu was low, Anne stayed in her room.

Karen turned. Stu was wiping up the counters on the other side of the kitchen, and for a moment she tensed. Sometimes he did task after despicable task as if to prove his worth. She hated the way he waited for her praise like a Boy Scout for a merit badge. But tonight he smiled, flipping the dishcloth over the faucet. "Hi, babe. You look like you walked home."

"Windblown?" she asked lightly. She would not let her eyes appraise him — he hated that.

"No, it's the color in your cheeks." He reached for her and she gave him a hug casually, cautiously, as she hugged any male friend. "All the kids want to see the same movie, believe it or not," he told her and his voice sounded hearty, alive. "What if we splurge on fast food and catch the early show?"

"Wendy's has baked potatoes and a salad bar," Anne reminded her from her perch. "You don't have to eat grease."

"Though you will," Karen remonstrated. "Sure, I guess we could." She looked at Stu, she couldn't help it. He seemed fine. He pulled her closer so she couldn't see. She put her arms around his neck, leaned against him just for a second of comfort. Reflexively, her arms tightened, her eyes closed; his arms were hard around her now, as if, no matter what, he wouldn't let go.

"Hurry up and get ready," Anne admonished them.

"It won't take much time," Karen replied, struggling to speak past Stu's soft, flannel shirt, to keep it light. She gave up, buried her face in his neck.

"Just a little more time, honey," Stu muttered into her ear, too low for Anne to hear. "That's all I need."

Two or three minutes passed before Karen wiggled free enough to kiss his jaw. "We have time," she said into his ear and lightly drew her tongue down its lobe.

THE LAST DAY
OF SPRING

L AURIE HAD WANTED FOR A LONG TIME TO VISIT JEN. When Mama took David, the baby, along to visit their favorite aunt, she and her older sister Carol had complained.

"I know you want to see her," Mama had explained, "but she's changed. I don't want you to see her like this. I don't think she does. David's so young he doesn't notice."

Today Mama was taking them but for the wrong reason. "I know it will be hard for you," she said when she asked them to get ready. Her voice was as raw and scratchy as stretched rope. "But you have to let her go. It will probably be easier for you if you see her."

"Why aren't you ready?" Mama said now. "Aunt Margaret will be here pretty soon." She sat down suddenly beside Laurie on the side of the bed. Laurie reached for her shoe. "I know you think I don't understand. You know, Laurie," she cleared her throat, "Margaret and Jim accepted this long before I did. So did Daddy. But I just couldn't . . . "

Laurie bent down to ease her heel into her shoe. Now Mama had made her throat hurt again, and she resented it, so she let Mama talk to the back of her neck and her curved shoulders.

"Maybe we're wrong, Laurie."

Laurie put on her other shoe and stood up. "But maybe we're not." She turned on one heel and talked over her shoulder the way Carol did sometimes. Carol would be a high school freshman in the fall. "I'm ready. And I want to visit her."

Laurie stopped for a moment at the mirror. She could feel Mama's eyes and moved so that her own image blocked her mother's reflection. Her hair was all right, smooth and shiny though not as dark and glossy as Carol's. Her pink dress looked fine with its V-neckline. Even her skinny legs looked better in nylon and low heels. She carefully applied the light lipstick Mama let her wear, blotted it, and rubbed the tissue on her cheekbones. Carelessly, she dropped the tissue into the small wastebasket by the closet and left the room.

Laurie had no intention of letting go. She knew that Jen would get well. She walked briskly out to the living room to watch out the picture window. Laurie heard stories about miracles and healings almost every Sunday. Every time as she sat listening hard, her knees clamped together but still trembling, she could see that Jen too, Jen for sure, would get well. David got better, and they had really been anxious about him.

The day David visited Jen, Daddy had picked up Laurie at her junior high to drive her to her clarinet lessons. He told her how David perched on Jen's bed and sang "You Are My Sunshine." He'd learned it from one of Mama's old records.

"David's were the only dry eyes in the room by the time he sang, 'Please don't take my sunshine away,'" Daddy said. "I don't know if you realize it, Laurie, but we almost lost David when he had pneumonia last winter."

Laurie nodded. She could feel that odd trembling in her knees. "Jen wanted the drapes pulled back, and since it was about two-thirty, the sun just blazed through the windows. They look west. David was right in the brightest square of sun on the bed."

Laurie could visualize him there, his blue eyes flashing with delight at being the center of a circle of adults.

"Then Jen said, 'I wish I could see him better.' She was laughing and wiping her eyes and didn't see the look your mother gave me. But now we know she is going blind."

Laurie jumped when Aunt Margaret rang the doorbell. Laurie could tell by the way she greeted Mama and lifted her eyebrows at Carol and Laurie that Aunt Margaret thought it a mistake to take them but wasn't going to say anything. Her own children hadn't visited Jen.

Laurie watched Mama and Aunt Margaret walk out to the car. They looked young and pretty with their white bags and shoes, the spring sunshine on their hair. She and Carol wore their Easter dresses with last year's summer shoes that pinched a little. It was warm this morning. No one needed a sweater.

On the way to the hospital Carol chatted with Aunt Margaret about Sylvia, the cousin Carol's age. No one said anything about Jen. Laurie felt that she could run faster than the car was moving, race it to the hospital and get there first. There were a hundred things she had to tell Jen. She wanted to interrupt Mama and say, "Even if Jen can't see well now, will she want to talk to us? Will she want to know what we've been doing? Can I say . . . ?" But it sounded stupid even in her own head so she kept still. She didn't know how the three of them could act as if they were going shopping or out to lunch.

Any other year they'd already be looking forward to the 4th of July party at Jen's. Sometimes several parties came first as if no one could wait. On the 4th there would be a barbecue on the patio. Everyone would sit in lawn chairs and on blankets eating from paper plates. The little cousins would race and tumble over each other, kicking cups of lemonade and squashing their toes into abandoned ice cream cones.

After dinner the oldest girls always huddled in one of the cars, playing the radio, talking, and shrieking with laughter.

Carol and Sylvia watched enviously, pretending not to notice. Maybe this year they would be old enough to get into the car.

Jen's husband, Al, usually found a shady corner and stretched out on the grass, his hat over his eyes. All the clamor and talk drifted over him like a cloud of gnats. The two oldest boys played catch on the far edge of the long side yard, endlessly throwing a softball back and forth, warning the younger boys to stay out of range.

Then when it was dark, too dark to play, Al would light the fireworks — flares, fountains, Roman candles, and rockets. They would all sit in groups on the lawn, watching the gleaming showers of sparks float shimmering and singly down through the warm, cricket-noisy air to melt in the black grass.

Laurie sighed and rolled down the window a little, not quite enough to blow Carol's hair. She listened to Aunt Margaret for a moment to see if they were saying anything about Jen, but they were talking about Aunt Margaret's next door neighbors. Their daughter was getting married, and Aunt Margaret's youngest daughter was going to be the flower girl. Aunt Margaret had been sewing her dress.

Laurie had often seen a wedding dress glistening like a ghost in the hall between the bedrooms in Jen's house. Jen often made them for the daughters of close friends or relatives.

"I want you to make my girls' wedding dresses someday," Laurie heard Mama say once as she stood admiring the white creation in the hall.

Jen smiled and shook her head. "You'll want to make them yourself."

Laurie rolled down the window another inch. Mama and Aunt Margaret were still talking about the wedding, and Carol was listening closely. She wondered if Al would be visiting Jen at the same time they did. Laurie felt a hollow in her stomach. Suddenly she missed Al almost as much as she had missed Jen. She didn't dare ask about Al though.

Al had a shop in the basement of his house. He drove a big black van, and all the children loved to clamber over his plumbing tools and peek out through the small rear window. Children were seldom allowed in Al's shop downstairs, but once when Laurie went down she saw a bed there. She wondered about that, if Al actually became so weary working in the shop that he couldn't climb up the stairs to the white double in Jen's bedroom.

Once on Thanksgiving the entire family hugged their chairs around Jen's train of white-clothed tables placed end to end through the living room and dining room. As they looked toward Al at the end of the row, he slowly sank from sight. He landed, they found by leaning from their own chairs, on his side still in his chair on the floor. After the concerned exclamations and a little suppressed laughter, Al picked himself up and a Thanksgiving blessing was said.

As the dishes began traveling up and down the sides of the tables, the teasing and laughter rose again. Then Jen said drily to Al, "I asked you to fix that chair months ago."

Everyone laughed uproariously, but when Laurie looked at Jen she saw that she was not laughing, and Laurie's own grin felt stiff. Jen was watching Al, who went on heaping his plate with food.

It was bad enough to have the summer ruined, Laurie thought bitterly as they turned on State Street, but what if Jen wasn't well in time for Christmas? Most Christmases Al made something wonderful for at least one age group of cousins. She and Carol had in their bedroom duplicate doll bunk beds and wooden cupboards with glass windows.

From Halloween on, visits to Jen and Al's house were almost torturous as adults were spirited away to the basement and returned with bright, secretive eyes. No child was allowed past the pantry above the basement stairs.

One year everyone received wooden turtles with wheels

on the underside, and they raced down the frozen sidewalks yelling and falling off. Last Christmas had been quieter, but the year before there were huge toy chests for the boys. Daddy and Uncle Jim carried in the first one. As they set it in the center of the living room floor, one of the twins leaped out with a rebel whoop. The shrieks of the girls, the crying of little Judy, and the loud, free laughter from the grownups still echoed in Laurie's head as Aunt Margaret said, "Well, here we are," and Mama set the brake on the car.

The inside of the county hospital seemed dim. The green walls shone faintly, but the floors were dull. Jen had been moved here a week ago because the months of hospital treatment had depleted her insurance and bank accounts. Mama had explained that to them last Saturday, adding that she and Aunt Margaret couldn't fill all the hours of constant care Jen needed now with friends and relatives. They hired a private nurse.

After she told about the nurse, Mama paused and added, "If Al comes by sometime and neither Daddy nor I are home, I don't want you to let him in."

Carol and Laurie exchanged startled looks. Carol pressed for more information; Laurie was outraged. Mama wouldn't say much but made them promise just the same.

"Al is a little different than we thought. Maybe because he's upset and worried."

Carol and Laurie could see her sorting through her thoughts like playing cards, sifting most back into the pile, turning a few face down on the table, and turning up several for them to see.

"Jen finally asked us not to schedule Al to stay with her because he would just leave, and then she didn't have anyone there." She hesitated again. "He changed the locks," she said at last and her voice trembled a little. "We used to go by Jen's house once in a while and pick up things Jen wanted. He changed the locks. And there have been other things. We just want you to be careful even if you don't understand."

Now Mama and Aunt Margaret paused before a door and spoke briefly to a nurse who was leaving the room. Laurie stopped just inside the door, realizing in time that she had missed hearing that they were going to visit someone else first. She waited politely for them to finish with this friend of Aunt Margaret's or great-aunt-whoever. She hoped they would hurry.

Then Laurie noticed that everyone except the woman in the bed was staring at her oddly. Carol seemed embarrassed as if Laurie were a child about to throw a public tantrum. Annoyed, Laurie smiled and stepped forward, waiting to be introduced. Then she realized with a jolt like the night she stuck her finger into an empty light socket in the dark that she knew this old, thin woman.

"Hi, Jen," she said and moved toward the bed, ready to gulp the words back if she was wrong.

The woman didn't answer, but now, standing beside her, Laurie could see that she had Jen's cheekbones and chin, her long straight arm and broad hand. The skin stretched over her bones like old tissue paper, grayed with delicate dust. Her hair was also gray and drawn back from her face. There was a transparent tube in one nostril. Her stillness was the stillness of stone.

"Mmmm, pretty flowers," said Aunt Margaret cheerfully. She looked at the card. "Adria sent them, I see. Pretty red tulips, aren't they Ruth?"

"Lovely," Mama answered. "You look better today, Jen. It's warm and beautiful outside."

Carol and Laurie looked at each other desperately across the bed. Neither could speak.

"Carol and Laurie wanted to come," Mama said, "so I brought them along. They're out of school now and bored already."

Carol managed a short laugh. Laurie tried to echo it but only squeaked. Horrified, she covered it with a cough and looked away.

She saw a card on the inside of the door, mounted with tape. It said, "Dear friends and family. Please remember that as far as we know, Jen still hears well. Govern your conversations accordingly." She looked back at Jen. Jen's hand was just inches from her own. She wanted to touch it, but she was too frightened. Jen's fingers were curled in as if she were holding something.

Once when Jim, Jr. and Mike were throwing a softball back and forth, Jen passed them on her way to the patio. She suddenly stepped in front of Jim, Jr. and caught the ball with a quick upward swing of her arm. She fired it to Mike as everyone cheered, and Jen bowed and bowed, shaking her stinging hand.

"Dorothy and Sam called from California," Mama said sweetly, smiling at Carol and Laurie. "They send their love. She said they think of you all the time and pray for you every night."

A croak came from the bed. Laurie jumped. It came again, a noise that might emerge from someone deaf from birth who had never heard the texture of a human voice nor been trained to imitate it. Mama and Aunt Margaret bent over Jen, no longer casual.

"Margaret?" Aunt Margaret said. "Do you want me to stay with you this afternoon?"

The noise came again. Jen's lips barely parted, there was no motion in her face or throat, yet Laurie could see the cords in her neck sharpen into ridges. She wanted to run.

"That's not it," Mama said.

"Miriam!" Margaret exclaimed. The sound stopped. "You want Miriam to come? That's it, isn't it? I'll call her this afternoon. I'm sure she'll come."

Jen was silent for the rest of the visit. Laurie was silent, too, staring at Jen then looking away. The only other person she had ever seen so motionless was her grandfather in his coffin. Yet, although Jen looked far less lifelike, Laurie was reminded by Jen of a jungle cat in the zoo, its eyes open only a silent slit, its powerful limbs indifferent. She hates having us see her like this, Laurie thought.

Laurie remembered that once last summer Jen had stayed in bed during one party and lay on the chaise lounge most of the others. Once when Jen started to go after something, Aunt Margaret said, "Lie down. You're supposed to be resting."

Suddenly Laurie remembered the most amazing thing in Jen's house of wonders — her clock. She had brought it home with her from a trip back east. It was electric with a gold rim and hands, but there was only air where the face should be, not even notches along the rim to mark the numerals. Laurie had thought the clock very odd and fascinating, but now in this brief, endless visit she thought that all clocks should be like Jen's. She thought the clock should be here in this room with Jen and nearly mentioned it. But Mama and Aunt Margaret were kissing Jen and leaving the room with Carol.

"Good-bye, Jen," Carol said.

Laurie walked to the end of the bed. She looked hard at Jen. Even at Christmas Jen had seemed well enough, sitting on the floor with the kids singing Christmas carols, the parents behind them on the sofa and overstuffed chairs. Laurie had glanced back quickly at Jen in the middle of a carol and caught her with tears in her eyes. Jen had grinned, and Laurie pretended not to notice the tears. She remembered them now though as she left Jen's room. She didn't say good-bye.

When they walked out of the hospital doors, the street seemed altered. Laurie remembered the ride home from the hospital after her appendectomy when she was ten. During those lost two weeks the leaves had turned and fallen. Now the city shimmered with the heat and hues of summer. A child with only basic colors in her crayon box had colored the grass strong deliberate green, the sky a relentless blue, and the sunlight so yellow she could almost see the crooked black smile crayoned on the sun's round face. The vivid red, orange, and violet flowers in the hospital garden burned her eyes.

Aunt Margaret wanted Mama to drop her off downtown to have her glasses adjusted. They talked of ordinary things, but the back of Mama's neck looked strained. Carol seemed uncertain, dabbing at her eyes. Laurie was amazed that Mama had taken them. She thought she could see something of what it had cost her in the set of her shoulders as she drove and the deliberate way she avoided their eyes in the rear view mirror.

"I'm positive she was asking for Miriam," Aunt Margaret said.

After a minute Mama said, "You're probably right."

"Miriam tells her she's going to get well. She wants her to come and tell her that again."

Laurie listened intently, but Mama seemed to be concentrating on the traffic. Laurie stared out the side window. It was easier now. The colors in the heart of town were dusty, softer.

"Hey, there's Al," she said sitting up straight. "Look— there! He's going into that restaurant with that lady."

They all looked, Mama's foot braking instinctively. A man with brown, thinning hair and long arms like Al's was holding the elbow of a young, red-haired woman. They disappeared behind the tinted glass door.

Carol and Laurie looked at each other and read mutual question marks. They listened expectantly. Mama changed lanes to turn the corner.

"That could be anyone," Margaret said. "Al is a very average man." Carol was leaning forward the way she did when she found out about square roots or spontaneous combustion. Then her face shut, and she sat back sedately.

Laurie slumped down in the back seat and began chewing on her thumbnail. She could see the whole afternoon stretched out before her like a blank inch on a road map. It was her turn to fix dinner and set the table. Carol's turn for family prayer. Laurie suddenly knew that Carol would pray for Jen's suffering to end and that she, Laurie, would refuse to say amen.

That night Laurie lay motionless in bed waiting for Carol to go to sleep. She startled as Carol slid with a thump from the bunk above her, swept her robe around her, sobbing, and burst out of the bedroom. In a minute or two Laurie heard Mama's voice, mingled with Carol's, the two of them talking brokenly. She could even see them through the closed white door, arms around one another. The lift of relief and acceptance in the voices tightened her throat. Her cheekbones ached. They had ached forever.

For a second it was almost too much for her. In the arches of her feet she could feel herself spring from the bed and run from the bedroom in her bare feet and summer nightgown into the peace of the eye that was opening in the storm. Then the jumbled voices clarified for a moment, and she thought she heard Mama say, "We have to let her go."

Laurie gripped the covers tightly and held on, glaring up at the springs of the top bunk and thinking of bitter, biting things to say to Carol when she returned to bed.

Laurie didn't know she had fallen asleep until she woke up sitting erect with tears dripping from her jaw. The house was dark and silent. The bunk above her sagged in the center. She sat there a moment, gasping and trembling, before the dream returned.

She was wearing a swishy yellow-dotted swiss dress Mama made the summer she was nine. It was after church — Sunday evening. They were running through the twilight across Jen's green hill of a front lawn, snatching up pods fallen from the maples and prying them open to press the sticky sides of the Y's against their noses. Then they ran past Al, stepping nimbly, lightly, over his hands outstretched above his head as he lay on the grass. He grabbed at their ankles, and they shrieked and ran on laughing, laughing.

The ache in her cheekbones eased as more tears washed over them, and kneeling flat on her legs she bent from the waist over her arms pressed hard against her stomach and cried into the nightgown bunched over her knees. She cried for the singularity of the childhood she had lost and for all the things she thought she had understood and was now quite sure she would never understand.

PAYDAY

T HEY'RE ALL TOO HOT NOW," HEATHER SAID, MOTION-
ing to the transients.

"So why don't they just dump that stuff if they don't need
it?" Randal wondered, stepping with her up to the curb, his right
hand chummily gripping her arm just above the elbow. "Why is
he wearing his coat? Just stupid?"

Heather winced and dropped the subject. Stupid was not a
word she liked to hear, not any more. Randal pulled open the
heavy door of The Old Judge, his favorite lunch spot. Glancing
back, Heather noticed a young man with brawny shoulders bent
like a bull's pawing through a garbage can down the block. His
head was hidden under the swinging plastic door. Randal didn't
see him or the skinny young woman with a crooked haircut,
who waited to one side.

Heather's parents hadn't noticed the transients either when
they accompanied Heather to Salt Lake City after she decided to
go back to work. They'd been preoccupied with trying to convince her to stay with them in Logan.

Across the green plastic table now, Randal winked at her
and under the table his knee rubbed hers. "Know what?"

"What, Randal?"

"You're sweet. You even feel sorry for bums, don't you."

Heather picked up the menu. If Jessie were here, she would say, "He's only after one thing, Heather, then he'll be gone. They'll all be gone. And then what will you do?"

Heather opened the menu to erase the image of Jessie, her slim hands on her hips, her caramel-colored hair swinging as she talked. She was always sure.

Reading down the menu carefully, Heather decided to have the mini-chef salad and a small Coke.

"I bet Jessie's going to move out," she told Randal miserably. He looked at her, his head tipped.

"Jessie, my roommate," she prompted. "I bet she is."

"Why would she?" Randal asked uncomfortably, then flashed his teeth at the waitress. "What are you going to have, Heather?"

Heather, about to explain why she thought Jessie might move, stared for a second at him, then at the waitress. "I forgot. Just a second." She opened the menu again, her face flushing.

Randal laughed, embarrassed, and it was not a nice sound. He ran one hand through his thick, brown hair combed straight back. "I'll have the enchilada special and a Tab," he said.

As soon as Heather saw the mini-chef salad on the menu she remembered. "I'll have the mini-chef salad."

"Anything to drink?"

"Oh." She scanned the menu again. Now where was the list of beverages?

"She'll have a small Coke," Randal said wearily.

"Yes. That's right." She folded the menu and handed it to the waitress before Randal folded his. She smoothed her hair. From the corners of her eyes she could just see the bend at the end of her dark strands that had grown out but were still not as long as before. She closed her eyes for a few seconds. Her head ached but not badly. Over the loudspeaker, John Lennon was singing softly, "Imagine all the people, living life in peace . . . "

"What were you and Sam laughing about in the library this morning?" Randal drawled. "I saw you over there by the current clip files."

Heather stopped listening to Lennon, opened her eyes, and smiled, thinking of Sam. "I don't remember. Sam's funny."

Randal snorted. "Yeah, funny. I've been working on that county government story for three months, and this morning he almost blew it by coming out with a story on parks. The two overlap, dammit."

Heather said nothing. Before she would have known what to say. She might have taken Sam's side or she might have been doing the story on parks herself. She'd apprenticed on the city beat with Sam before her accident. The newspaper had hired her right out of Utah State University in Logan. Then, only six months after she became a reporter, she went snow tubing with some college friends over the Thanksgiving weekend. When they whirled out of control on the frozen hill and crashed, her head struck a tree.

That's what they told her. At least she could remember everything up to that weekend. When she had left the newspaper that Wednesday afternoon, she had filed what turned out to be her last story. The story ran on page B-1, a feature on transients trying to survive the cold weather. Salt Lake had not had this many transients before. They were tearing down an old park bandstand board by board and burning the boards under a freeway viaduct to keep from freezing.

She remembered following and writing the story, but she barely remembered the hospital or coming home after three weeks in a coma and three months in rehabilitation. Now she wasn't a reporter any more. Her mind seemed to snag or lose information at random. She worked in the newspaper's library, where the stories the reporters wrote could be cut out, stacked, mounted, and neatly filed, the information all contained. Yet she still noticed the transients.

Randal didn't care about transients. He was talking about county departments and which administrator wasted how much tax money. She let him talk, and when their lunches arrived she began to eat, nodding when he looked at her, watching how he timed his talk and breathing around bites of streaming red enchilada.

"Are you busy tonight?" Randal asked finally, scooping up the last of the sauce with his spoon.

Heather reached into her purse, gave him three dollars for her salad, then got out her appointment book. She turned the pages one by one.

"Today's May 9," Randal said. His voice reminded her of sweet and sour sauce.

"I know," she snapped. She placed her index finger on the number nine. "Yes, I am busy. Jessie and I have to go to her sister's birthday party."

"Jessie, Jessie. Come on, you don't want to do that."

"What do you want me to do?"

"Oh, I thought we might just kind of hang out, you know?" He winked. He did that a lot, Heather thought. "Maybe get something to eat."

"Well, I can't, Randal."

He took her hand. He looked into her eyes with his intent, black-fringed, green eyes. "Yes, you can, Heather. Please." He squeezed her hand, and she felt the hard bones in it soften from his warmth.

"I can't. I don't want to make Jessie mad."

He let go of her hand and drained his Tab noisily. "So you think she might move out. Is that why you have to give in to her?"

Heather suddenly felt cold. "Do you think she will?"

"Heather! You said earlier you think she might move out. I don't know."

"Oh. Well, I don't know either. She says she won't, but then later she says maybe she'll go away to graduate school. It's just a feeling I have."

What Jessie had really said was that she thought Heather needed to find someone who could be a good husband, who would take care of her. Jessie didn't want her to date guys like Randal.

Now he seemed mad. He grabbed the ticket and went to pay it while Heather fumbled in her wallet for a tip. She was always trying to surprise him with how efficient she could be. When he came back, he walked past her without looking to see if she followed him out. She caught up when they reached the sidewalk.

"Don't be mad, Randal."

"Who's mad?"

They walked back to the newspaper in silence. Heather had no words to counter him. Anyway, she knew he'd come in the library to see her when she stocked the big closet's back shelves that afternoon. And she knew she'd let him stay a little while, just for company.

Loretta ran the library, and she lost patience with Heather at least twice a day. When Heather forgot something or misunderstood Loretta's instructions, she tried to ask Ruthie or Georgia before Loretta found out.

That afternoon when Loretta gave Heather her paycheck, she looked at it, then at Heather for a long minute before letting go of the envelope. Heather had felt her fingers tighten, sure that Loretta would snatch it back.

Sam found Heather blinking back tears by the drinking fountain and led her around the corner. "Well, *she* doesn't pay you," he said when Heather told him. "She works for the newspaper just like we do."

"The thing is," Heather said, "I remember how it was at City Desk. I mean, I remember working with you and Lisa and Randal and everyone. I remember how it felt to do those stories, even the hard ones. But I just can't do it any more."

"But you're still recovering, right?" Sam asked gently. Sam had always been nice, even when they were in the middle of stories that were falling apart. He reminded Heather of John Lennon, especially Lennon's last few albums about people caring for each other. Sam was Jewish and John Lennon British, but they seemed to be brothers anyhow.

But even Sam's gentleness had altered somehow, and in its difference it resembled Randal's new intimacy and Loretta's new impatience. They were all mirrors that reflected the inside of Heather's head, not her dark hair and blue eyes, telling her how different she was now, how drastically life had changed.

At 4:30 Ruthie picked up her sweater and purse and said, "Well, Heather, I'm going to the bank. Don't you need to go, too?"

"Oh, yes. Thanks for mentioning it, Ruthie. What if I forgot?"

Ruthie's bank was in the mall, so Heather left her there and went through the double doors into the warm afternoon and crossed the street. She was only a few yards from her bank's granite steps when she saw another transient.

He was young, about Randal's age, with sandy, longish hair and a beard. His big hazel eyes were bloodshot in the corners. She felt his eyes on her face, then her body, and she looked down. She observed his feet, shoved into Oxfords that were split from the seam at the arch all the way back — totally without heels. The soles flapped like bedroom slippers as he walked toward her. When he raised an arm, Heather saw that his elbow protruded nakedly through the heavy jacket. Heather thought about the hard winter and the rainy spring.

"Extra change?" he mumbled, his eyes glancing off hers.

"No," she said, but her paycheck burned in the pocket of her purse. "I mean I'm just going to the bank. Can—can you wait a minute?"

The bank's interior was cool and dim. Her hand shook as she wrote out the deposit slip, adding an extra ten dollars to the cash she allowed herself. Was ten dollars too much for him? Was it enough to do any good? Would he drink it? Did it matter to her if he did? Then she had to stop thinking about the transient so she could do the subtraction and check it with addition.

By the time she made the deposit, put away her cash, and chatted with the cashier, she'd forgotten the transient even though urgency still hummed in her chest. But as she hurried down the slick stone steps, a rumpled body sprawled on the patch of grass out front reminded her of her errand. A hand on one bearded cheek propped his head, and he didn't look up.

As Heather hurried toward him, she noticed his bare ankles, exposed between the trousers, his bent knees drawn up and the rims of his shoes. The ankles looked bluish, bruised. Heather felt something inside her give way.

She stepped over the rail, sank to the grass beside the feet, and fumbled in her purse for her wallet. She unsnapped it and with shaking fingers found the bill. She found she couldn't speak but didn't know why until she saw water drop on her hand, then streak his dirty ankle as she bent toward him with the money. She dropped the money by his hand, sat back on her heels, and wiped off her wet cheeks.

But now the man was hunching his feet toward his body, his blue eyes staring stupefied at her face. With his elbows, he dragged himself away from her.

Next she heard voices nearby and looked up. Three teenagers waiting on the corner for the bus were watching. And now a scruffy young man with a beard, torn shoes, and one elbow poking from his jacket walked toward her as if he knew her, as if he expected something.

Heather looked back at the transient nearest her. His odor suddenly filled her nostrils as she realized she had made a mistake. She felt panic catch her, a familiar nightmare in which everything she did went wrong. She wondered if she could spare another ten dollars for the transient she had promised money.

A policeman, though, was brushing by the younger transient, walking toward Heather as the man beside her got to his feet, stepped over the fence, and hurried away. Looking up, Heather noted that the policeman was rather short, with sandy hair, a reddish face, and gray eyes. Policemen had to be responsible, Heather knew, but she did not think this one would make a good husband.

Still, she felt calmer, swallowing her tears, carelessly shaking back her hair. She smiled at the people collecting casually along the sidewalk, even the transient who stared back skeptically. "Imagine there's no heaven," she began to sing, her voice wavering in the noisy air so that she blushed and wished that she'd brought her guitar. Her hands still remembered chords even when she forgot the words. As she sang, she recalled John Lennon dying on the lobby floor. "Imagine all the people . . . living for today . . . "

The teenagers waiting for the bus smiled at her, their eyes curious and amused. She thought they might join in except for the policeman who was still staring down at her as if she were preaching in a foreign tongue or stripping or . . . She stopped singing.

His eyes had a flat look she had seen before. The memory burst into her brain, three dimensional. She and Sam had been checking a tip on supposed inhumane conditions at the zoo. As they talked over the little evidence they'd found, they watched two cobras behind glass, winding through each other's coils.

"They're like being a reporter," the Heather-before was saying. "Every story is important because an aware public might improve things, right? But at the same time, there's the plain fact that nothing ever really changes."

"So that means there's always another story," Sam had smiled, "but there's no story here."

Now, the Heather-after was left with the policeman who had cobra eyes and the cluster of people behind him. She picked herself up and smiled at him understandingly as she stepped back over the rail.

"You can't change a changing world," she confided. But she could tell from his set jaw, just beginning to open, that he had never seen the cobras she referred to. Also, he didn't care to know how her head ached.

COYOTE TRACKS

IT'S OVER," HE SAID. "I'M TELLING YOU, SHANNI, IT'S TIME
you quit running away."

"I'm not running away," Shannon said, pleased that her
voice sounded as smooth and more cheerful than Don's. He
seemed stressed and his old nickname for her had an alien tone.
"I'm living here. I have a job."

But after she hung up the telephone and checked Marci,
her daughter, curled up reading in bed, she left—hurrying from
the high school faculty quarters toward the moon's huge face,
walking in half light toward the road. There was still traffic at
9:00 p.m., tardy tourists turning off Highway 163 toward the
Gouldings Motel opposite the Tribal Park. Posh rooms would
welcome them, though the sun was down on one of the world's
most spectacular views. Europeans and Japanese paid well, Shannon had heard, for balconies facing the Monument Rocks. By
now, the dining room would be closed, and anyone who hadn't
eaten in Kayenta, Arizona, to the south or Mexican Hat, Utah,
to the north, was at the mercy of the Gouldings' convenience
store. There, Navajos were still shopping inside or gossiping

alongside their pickups in the lot. Still, no doubt, Ben Yazzie, Sammy Begay, and Nicholas Lee punched at the video games. She had greeted them there at 6:00 when she and Marci stopped by for a piece of microwaved pizza. The boys flashed quick grins backward, although their eyes never left the colored, jumpy screens.

The November wind was cold and the moon rising as she walked briskly toward the store and laundry next to it, then past, ignoring the turnoff to the motel. She pressed the soles of her hiking shoes into the still-soft, pink dust. She hadn't seen December here yet but knew from last January and February that once rain and snow came, the roads would alternate between frozen ruts and clay that gulped like quicksand. Shannon followed the road's curve toward Oljato—not that she could walk so far, but she didn't need a real destination. At any rate, Oljato was only a pink cliff sporting the town's name over a dusty housing development and an old trading post.

The wind, blowing women's voices and then a man's harsh laugh down from the motel parking lot, buffeted her straw hat. She had bought it, a true reservation hat, at the Tuba City Trading Post a month ago. She was letting her hair grow long, since the constant wind blew any short cut flat and stiff against her head like an old doll's hair. Maybe someday she would figure out how to do a Navajo knot, low on her neck. A streaky blond Navajo knot. Marci's hair was already long enough to braid and keep the wind out, and Marci's eyes had lost the scared look they had worn—since when? Since her parents had started fighting? Since the silence between them had grown? Since Shannon took Marci and relocated? Or did it go back even earlier to when Marci's baby brother had died—a time Shannon could barely remember except for her own pain. Oh, Marci had lost a lot, but she still had Shannon and Shannon still had her. So Don missed Marci now that his girlfriend Heidi was gone. Shannon scuffed the dust like talcum powder. She and Marci had healed over, they were learning to survive.

Shannon had become a walker here, that was another change; she learned not to pat Indian children on the head nor to point to the students she called on in class. No matter how long she stayed, she doubted she could point with her lips as the Navajos did, but she had broken herself of hand pointing. One didn't point a finger toward anything living, in fact, including the Rocks, the sun. Courtesy here was inclusive. She'd learned that the students who wouldn't meet her eyes had been taught to defer to authority — and age?

Her shoes were fast and slightly squeaky in the dust, her slender muscles grateful for the exercise after a long day in class. Don's voice, as familiar as a warm hand on her skin, had locked the tension into her bones. He had called twice so far this month. Thanksgiving and Christmas were coming, maybe that was it. They'd never spent holidays apart, but last year Marci had exclaimed a little too much over every gift she opened, had insisted that they both admire everything, play every game. By the end of the day, all their nerves were wrenched even though Heidi's name went unmentioned. Now Heidi had taken a position with the legal defenders in southern California, Don said.

So she can't handle your divorce, Shannon had replied, not sorry even for his shocked silence. Anger helped; it coated her like wax. Maybe he wanted them back, maybe not. She resisted even examining that question, for what he wanted first was the exquisite agony of discussing it all — again. And she didn't — she had left all that behind.

Walking faster, she let her eyes swallow moonlight, drowning her inner vision of Don's dark, curly hair, his hazel, questioning eyes, the lithe way he moved, so many years of being best friends and lovers. Why not let his voice trickle out of her ears, through the hat's weave, into the wind whirling east now, pursuing a sand devil. A gray horse twenty feet to her right snorted at the shift in breeze, turned its back, and shuffled toward other dark shapes.

Eighteen months ago when she'd become convinced Don was having an affair with Heidi, a clerk in his law office, Shannon had silently begun her preparations. She renewed her teacher's certification and sent her application. She opened a separate checking account and doubled the number of students she tutored. All of that she had done right, but when the split came — and Don seemed to think it was her idea — she had been unprepared for the pain. No one had told her that separation or divorce was an amputation. She felt half of Siamese twins once Don moved out, half a heart, half a brain, half as competent as she had been before. Maimed, she limped through fall and early winter until a second-semester job offer came from San Juan County, the farthest Utah county from Salt Lake City. She signed for English classes at Monument Valley High School because of the distance. Also, she'd heard the scenery was spectacular, and living in the Navajo Nation seemed almost like foreign travel. A new start, she told Marci, a lot of fun. Six months later, in July, they'd driven to Yellowstone to escape summer's worst heat on the reservation, visited in Salt Lake City, then to everyone's astonishment, returned to Monument Valley. Don, of course, objected to her taking Marci so far away again, but she never considered anything else. Besides, he had the fair-haired Heidi. She couldn't recall him mentioning Heidi during that visit, though; maybe the love affair was weakening even then.

Shannon was passing Ben Yazzie's home now, though the contrast of the blue trailer against the red mesa was lost to darkness. A hogan stood on one side of the frame house, on the other side a shade house, and thirty feet beyond, an outhouse. She half expected to hear Ben pounding down the road behind her, but probably the store hadn't closed yet. He'd still be playing The Avengers, his hands quick on the plastic triggers. That day in class Ben had been the first to raise his hand when she assigned the students a personal essay on the Monument Rocks directly across the highway from the high school. How did they feel watching the Rocks change color according to the weather? In what ways did the Rocks's famed beauty influence them or touch them? She completed her explanation and asked for questions. Ben's hand shot up. "What rocks?" he asked.

One of Ben's numerous cousins, Stanley Yazzie, lived next to her in the faculty compound. Stan, the school's football coach and counselor, was bigger than Shannon had known Navajos could be. In mild weather, she and Stan often sat on her front steps, watching Marci hunt grasshoppers in the weeds by the row of swings. If Marci caught one, she'd bring it for Stan's careful inspection, then they'd let it go.

Shannon knew from their leisurely conversations that Stan had long roots in Monument Valley, the son and grandson of medicine men. All through junior high and high school, however, he'd lived in a Mormon home in Salt Lake City. She could picture him — a shadow at summer ceremonies, gradually learning the complicated sings, then in winters wearing a white shirt and sport coat to pass the sacrament in the red brick chapel in the city. He'd gone to Brigham Young University on a football scholarship, earned a secondary teaching certificate, and then come home to stay. By then his grandfather was so infirm that he was confined to his hogan next to the family trailer. Stan had cared for his grandfather and learned parts of three sings, but he wasn't considered a medicine man. Once in a while he attended meetings at the Mormon ward in Kayenta, Shannon knew, but not often. She and Marci went with him on Easter Sunday, but Shannon had lost the churchgoing habit soon after she married Don.

"We had a peach tree beside a grapevine down in the canyon where we took the sheep every summer," Stan had explained that Easter evening, his broad hands eloquent. "Gradually the vine grew up the tree and through the branches. We couldn't get it out. For years we picked both grapes and peaches from the tree while we waited to see which would strangle the other. Sometimes I think I am probably like that tree. That may be why my wife has gone back to live with her people at Navajo Mountain. Or maybe it is only that I have to live by the football field and she is a Navajo Mountain girl. She wants our boys to grow up there."

Shannon had nodded, but even now she didn't understand. He seemed so fitted to the school, the red earth, the students who teased him affectionately in the halls. Why would his wife prefer Navajo Mountain? That village was so remote that Shannon had never visited there. Walking faster, she wondered whether the peach tree or the grapevine had withered first.

She knew that the green football field was exactly what Ben Yazzie saw outside the high school, not the red stone monoliths just beyond. Shannon would have to read her students' essays when she went home. Marci would probably be asleep, the book upside down on her chest, her stuffed Garfield cat staring at the low ceiling. Marci's school bus to Halchita stopped for the compound's children at 7:30. Once Marci was fed and combed, she snatched her lunch sack and homework and hopped down the compound steps to pick up her best friend, Angela, who was teaching her Navajo words and phrases. Angie's father, Jim, taught wood shop at the high school and her mother, Margie, directed the school lunch program. Marci and Angie lived at each other's homes. Shannon watched their friendship with satisfaction and a little envy. After Marci left each morning, Shannon had half an hour to run the breakfast dishes under the hot water tap, dress, and organize her day before hurrying down the hill to the high school. She and Marci were both quick these days. Living without Don was surprisingly uncomplicated, or was it living on the reservation? At any rate, there seemed less reason to fuss.

Now that she thought it time for separation to become divorce, did Don think it was time that separation become marriage again? Six months ago he had shouted that any breakup ought to be final. She felt she would die from the violence in his voice. Shannon startled as a rabbit dashed in front of her almost clipping her shoe, then vanished into the sage. Was a coyote close behind? She paused but nothing moved. Her eyes rose to the sky, now plastered with stars like roses on wallpaper. Coyote had done that, she knew, from her book of Navajo mythology. Impatient Coyote, who couldn't wait for the pattern to be completed, the balance to be achieved.

"Coyote is not always bad," Stan had explained when he found her reading in her classroom at noon while munching a tuna sandwich. "He is the trickster, the catalyst. He's the surprise, but for Navajos, often surprise is bad. Hozros is the ideal." Coyote was not showing himself tonight, but Shannon could imagine his sharp muzzle behind a thick clump of yucca.

Hozros, beauty, harmony. She rubbed her cold cheeks hard, quickening her stride again. She was passing Sarah Atene's hogan and corrals. Sarah, a weaver who demonstrated her art for the school's culture club, would never allow her shiny-haired granddaughter to go walking like this, Shannon knew. A young Navajo girl out alone was, still considered fair game. But a bilagáana like herself, especially one past thirty, would not be bothered, probably not even by the Johnson brothers who liked to drink and roar up and down the dirt roads in their rusty, maroon pickup. Don, of course, would be outraged to know she was walking reservation roads alone at night, risking God-knows-what in the way of accident or assault, leaving Marci alone in her bed. She should protect Don's property — herself and Marci — better, she thought wryly.

Shannon had heard the car approaching from a long way back. Probably a Navajo driver, judging from the moderate speed. Not unexpectedly, it slowed more as it drew close. A

Navajo driver would be curious to see who was out at night. Not until the car stopped was she alarmed and then not overly.

"Yah-ta," she said quickly, straining her eyes past the headlights.

"It's me, Stan." Of course. She could see the outlines now of his blue Datsun. "I'm just out driving. Want a ride around Oljato and back?"

"Oh, I need the walk back." Then she changed her mind. "All right." She climbed in deciding she was more weary than she thought.

He pressed the accelerator, and they drove along slowly. She watched the moon as he braked for livestock near the road and the always foolhardy rabbits and ground squirrels. He drove as easily as he kept silence. She wondered if he had seen her leave the compound. Was he really just out driving, led to her by her thoughts? Synchronicity, Nadine, her astrologer friend in Salt Lake City, would call it. In synch, Don would say, snapping his fingers.

Stan braked quickly, reaching across her protectively as a rabbit streaked out from under the car. "I love the way you're so careful of the critters," Shannon told him, as he drove on.

"Their people have been here as long as mine have," Stan said, "maybe longer. Longer than the cars and trucks, that's for sure. Longer than the road."

"Maybe so," Shannon teased, "but they've never learned about the right-of-way."

"Why should we have the right-of-way?" Stan shrugged. "It's the nature of a rabbit or a squirrel to run, the nature of a horse to browse along. Isn't it the nature of vehicles to slow down or stop just as much as to speed along fast?"

"I guess," Shannon said, distracted by the square window lights of Oljato, frame houses all in rows. Tonight she couldn't see the dirt yards, a few with yellowing grass, but a satellite dish

ahead beamed back their headlights. Oljato's residents had elec-
tricity, running water, bathrooms as did Shannon. Still, she admired the lone hogan nestled under a spectacular cliff. Hogans,
though, didn't have windows. There was privacy.

"Quit looking, you voyeur!" Don would tease, when they
drove through the city at night, but she couldn't help herself.
She loved to watch people in their lighted windows, so peaceful
as they went through the tired motions of living. She'd never
seen anything obscene or unusual, just a head bent over a desk,
graceful arms reaching into high cabinets, children whirling to
silent music, old people criss-crossing a golden dining room. It
did her good, that lamplit domesticity. Hozros.

They droned slowly past the town and the pavement ended.
The dirt road would jounce them more slowly around the mountain to Gouldings. Now that she was in the car, she wondered
about Marci—was she worried? Had she fallen asleep yet? But
to turn and retrace the paved road would take nearly as long,
and she didn't want to see the same route twice. She decided to
say nothing. When the road slanted upward and turned, she
whirled in the seat, looking back.

Shannon thought Stan smiled in the darkness as he braked
so she could see better. "Moon-reflected-in-water," he said. "I
told you the meaning of Oljato a long time ago."

"Yes, but I never saw any water around." Oljato, painted
on the pink mountain, seemed to herald the most arid spot on
the reservation. But here in a rectangular pond the moon swam,
huge and limpid. She got out of the car and stared until shivers
made her climb back in. Rushing her would not occur to Stan.

The engine purred and they bumped along the dirt road.
"Troubles?" Stan asked finally. So he had seen.

"In a way. Don called. He wants Marci to come up for
Thanksgiving and Christmas."

"Mmmm."

They were silent for a few minutes, then Shannon asked, "What happens down here on the holidays? I don't suppose you celebrate Thanksgiving, do you?" She laughed.

"Sure." His teeth shone as he grinned. "Any excuse for a big feast. No one much stays at the high school. Those who do get together. Christmas, everyone goes to family. Myself, I go to Navajo Mountain if I can make it over the dirt road. If the road freezes or there is not too much snow."

Shannon decided to drop the subject and her worry with it. She wanted to take home with her the mood she had fled into the darkness to capture. She watched the moon, the silent shacks and hogans. With her window halfway down, she could hear sheep bells, dogs yipping, silence. The road smoothed out—paved again. They passed the KOA Campground and the brick houses built for the medical staff at the Seventh Day Adventist hospital. Too soon they were through the split cliffs, passing the Gouldings motel headed toward the store and the high school. "Could you let me off here?" she asked Stan before the car turned off the road. "Thanks."

"Good night, friend," he said.

Walking toward the compound, she breathed in the night. Her footfall became tuned again to the cliffs' low hum and her hands fell as uncaring as the wavering bushes. Before entering the compound, she turned and looked toward the hills. The old ones had lived behind the stone walls beneath the cliffs' overhang— the bird people, her mythology book said for who else could build homes so high? They had slept within reach of the wind. She closed her unlocked front door, smoothed the sheet over her daughter's thin legs, and turned out Marci's light; she bathed quickly in the dark bathroom, crawled nude into bed and slept.

A rare male rain beat at the windows of Shannon's classroom during lunch hour. Occasionally her hand stole into her lunch sack. She slowly chewed an apple; blindly her hand found a miniature candy bar left from Halloween, her eyes in her book. She was not even a hundred pages into the complicated worlds of the Diné, but, as she pored over the paragraphs, her astonishment grew. Surprisingly, First Woman, hoping to bond men and women, had created sexual pleasure. Not sex or procreation — the Diné were already producing offspring. No, sexuality itself, intended to delight and fulfill both men and women. From turquoise First Woman fashioned a penis and from white and red shell a vagina and clitoris. Then, before the watching village, she had placed her creations on the ground and taught them to respond to one another. Obediently, the organs had lengthened, each at the thought of the other, and then they had learned to shout. Only when their shouts were both strong had First Woman bestowed her gifts upon a boy and girl who had come of age.

Then as the sky swooped and the earth rose in an embrace, Coyote had bounded forward, blowing his plucked chin whiskers between the youths' legs. All had agreed that this addition was most attractive — so attractive, First Woman decided, that both men and women had better clothe themselves in the presence of others. Sexuality, fidelity, temptation, and modesty thus were born.

Shannon dropped her lunch sack into the wastebasket and walked over to the window to stare out at the rain. She imagined decades of Victorian prudery, Christian preaching, and the Kinsey Report bobbling in puddles on the resilient red clay. She shook her head and opened her book on the window sill, reading faster.

Sex had not made matters simple, she found, despite its delights, for after a time First Woman and First Man had quarreled and separated, with the men following First Man across the river. After several years of frustrated longing, people began to abuse themselves. One maiden, lost in her desire for a man, had found an antler; another maiden one day discovered a stout eagle feather; a third whittled a cactus smooth and fleshy; and the fourth maiden selected a long stone. Each had warmed the object all day in the sun, then spent an entire night evoking shouts from her bijóózh. Shannon reread those paragraphs; they were amazingly sensual. After First Man and First Woman reconciled and the people intermingled again, the four maidens gave birth to frightening monsters, the penalty for making a mockery of marriage.

The bell rang and the students noisily came in and took their seats. The rain had everyone astir, it seemed. Shannon asked Mary Holliday to begin reading the fifth chapter of *The Pearl*, knowing that Mary would read smoothly, while Shannon collected her thoughts. Most children came to school speaking Navajo and not until third grade or so did they become fluent in English; that, plus the teacher turnover and poor attendance due to distance and ceremonies, kept their grade test scores below average. Her students fetched water, fed livestock, or took the pickup out to gather wood after school. Sacrifice enough, many parents felt, to allow their children nine idle months behind desks staring at chalk marks on a green board, without encouraging more studying at home.

"Thank you, Mary," Shannon said. "Jeanette?"

She watched Jeanette's dark hair swing back as she lifted the book. She'd heard that Jeanette's younger sister, Mabel, had recently had her kinaalda, the ceremony to initiate womanhood. In high school, Shannon mused, she had considered her bijóózh once a month and then unhappily. She'd had only the vaguest notion that it could shout but a strong sense that it must be protected, even above her life. Later, of course, when she and Don married at twenty, her bijóózh seemed suddenly her most valuable part — not only to Don but to the gynecologist she had to see, maybe even to the Sunday school president who kept flirting with her, certainly to the women in her Mormon ward. They were all intent on the particulars of conception, miscarriage, and birth. They made only a rare, veiled allusion to sexual pleasure but referred scornfully to adultery and fornication. The woman who was most vocal on the subject of confessing sexual sin to the bishop, Shannon remembered suddenly, had been married to the Sunday school president.

But Navajo girls grew up with female and male gods stationed on every mountain, with misty female rain and driving male rain, even with male and female hogans. These girls whose Navajo tongues clicked and hissed in the restroom, whose hair and eyes shone, surely must know from childhood just how they got their bijóózhs and why. The cautionary tales forbidding masturbation also indicated that desire was natural and powerful and promised joy. Some Navajo girls got pregnant in their teens, but then so had practically a quarter of Shannon's graduating class, and those she knew hadn't even enjoyed it. "Thank you, Jeanette," she said with a sigh. "Ben?"

That afternoon, as Shannon waited at the bus stop for Marci, she seriously considered an invitation from Betsy Cairn, the Spanish teacher. That morning Betsy had invited Shannon to spend Saturday evening with her, Dick Jones, the math teacher, and a few teachers from White Horse High School in Montezuma Creek. "We're going to get Mexican food in Bluff," Betsy said, her green eyes snapping, "and just go on from there."

She must have looked dubious, because Betsy added, "Come on, Shannon. It's healthy to loosen up once in a while."

So Shannon laughed and shrugged, excusing, "I'm only separated. I really haven't started going out."

"Come off it, girl. We've got to get you around some Anglo men." Shannon blushed at Betsy's wink but didn't pursue the subject. Had other teachers noticed how frequently Stan dropped by her classroom or went walking with her? After all, he lived right next door. "Well, maybe you're right," she'd told Betsy offhandedly. "Dick's gone on you, obviously. What are the others like?"

"Oh, you've got to meet Fred. He teaches science at White Horse High. I think you'll like him. Let me know, okay?"

Marci jumped off the school bus, her short braids bouncing, and Angie right behind her. "Come on, rascal," she said, steering Marci around a small pool that now reflected blue sky. "How would you like to spend Saturday night with Angie?"

"Terrific," Marci said, sidestepping one puddle and kicking through the next, spattering red clay up her legs and on to Shannon's shoes.

"I have to talk with Jim and Marge first," Shannon warned.

"Call them up, Mom. I can't wait. We have to make plans. This is my first overnighter since we came here."

"Mine too," Shannon thought, and smiled guiltily. Of course it wouldn't be an overnighter; she hardly knew these people. But she whistled under her breath as she dialed the Thomases' number.

Shannon was nervous all day Saturday, especially after Marci packed her pillow, sleeping bag, and Barbie dolls down to Angie's that afternoon. She showered and washed her hair way too early, then tried on nearly all the clothes in her closet, finally ending up in a white sweater with metallic gold thread in the weave. Her straight denim skirt had zipped slits front and back. She zipped each half way.

Betsy arrived at 6:45 in a black leotard, skintight jeans, and a white leather jacket. "It pays to advertise," Don used to say when he saw a woman dressed that provocatively. Shannon wondered if Stan had seen Betsy come in and guessed what they were up to—but what did it matter if he had? Anyway, a loud rhythmic pounding came from his apartment through the wall. She couldn't imagine what *he* was up to.

"I had to zip up my jeans with pliers," Betsy confided cheerfully.

"You look great," Shannon said lamely.

"We're stopping by for Dick, then taking his car. What's the matter?"

"Oh, just before you came, Marge Thomas called. Marci just threw up her dinner. I'm going to have to bring her home."

Betsy glared a minute, then placed a sleek hip on the back of the sofa. "You're a lousy liar, Shannon. What is it? You're chickening out?"

"I guess I am. I'm just not up to it. Maybe I'm more married than I think."

"Look, it's just dinner out. That's all. Maybe we'll go back to Fred's house in Montezuma Creek. He's the only guy who doesn't have to make priesthood meeting in the morning."

"Next time," Shannon said. "Really."

"Okay, kid," Betsy relented. "Don't say you're not wanted. It's going to take some fancy footwork now to get a date for Fred."

"Sorry, Bets. Have fun. I'll go next time."

After Betsy left, Shannon flopped backwards full length on the couch. She thought she was going to throw up. Betsy was right—she was inhibited. She'd married Don so young—she hadn't any experience with being single, drinking and partying, deciding when and whether to go home with whom. When it came right down to it, she couldn't imagine herself moving that fast from an introduction into bed, and she knew that was where the evening was likely to lead. Had Don learned to do it by now? She guessed he had although Heidi had been right in his office, bright, pretty, no doubt a good listener. Theirs had been a relationship, she admitted. Even Marci had liked Heidi. She closed her eyes, realizing that the pounding next door had stopped, then heard Stan shout through the wall, "Are you sick?"

Shannon sat up. She'd never realized the walls were so thin and wondered now if she'd ever shouted at Marci. "No," she yelled back, adding, "Have you taken up head bumping or what?"

She couldn't hear him laugh but guessed that he did. "I'm coming over," he called then. "Is that okay?"

Rezipping her skirt, she answered, "Sure, why not?" Usually the three of them watched television or played Clue if the static was too bad. One time Marci had talked Shannon into teaching Stan how to make fudge. They got into a straw blowing contest and the fudge turned sugary, but still good. Shannon forgot the nervousness in her stomach as she headed for the door. She found Stan outside with his hands full of pulpy leaves and a hammer between his teeth. He was alone. She took the hammer.

"Does your dentist recommend this?"

"Nope. I'm making shampoo."

"Oh! Yucca shampoo? I've heard about washing hair with yucca — at the kinaaldas, right?"

"Or after a death. Any time."

"It must take a lot of pounding."

"Sure does. This stuff is almost done, though. You got a bread board?"

She did. She watched him pound, and then they boiled the pulp and strained it.

He looked her over speculatively. "I guess you already washed your hair?"

"I did."

"Someday I'll wash it for you."

Was he serious? She smiled and said nothing.

"But you didn't go out. Aren't you hungry?"

"Starving. Let me see what's in the fridge."

"Marci's away?" he asked. She glanced back over her shoulder but he had opened the overhead cupboards, surveying the canned goods at his eye level. Oh, he had her evening all surmised.

"She's at Angela's. They've been begging for an overnighter."

"Mmmhmm."

She blushed, glad to rummage through the vegetable drawer another moment. "I was going out to dinner with Betsy and Dick and their friends and figured I might be a little late getting back."

When Shannon stood and turned around, Stan was poking into the next cupboard. "Did you know you have enough spaghetti in here to feed Halchita? I make terrific spaghetti."

"You do? I bet I don't use as many pans." That was an old dig at Don.

"I'll wash the pans," he said. "Get out of my way."

"What if I fix a salad?"

"What did you do, get rich?"

"No, but I found some decent lettuce at the store yesterday, and I still have some peppers and tomatoes I bought in Kayenta last week."

"Well, salad's not traditional but okay."

They both laughed. For a second Shannon thought Stan was going to reach out a long arm and hug her. Navajos weren't much for hugging, she knew, but she felt hugged. She turned away and opened the refrigerator, stooping for green onions pushed back on the bottom shelf.

"I sure like that skirt."

"Oh, thanks. I guess I ought to change if I'm going to stay home and cook."

"Why? You won't dress up for me?"

"Well, this isn't really dressed up . . . " She stopped in confusion.

"Not like Betsy, you mean?" His teeth flashed in his brown face again. "You look better. Wait a minute—don't you have any tomato paste?"

"I thought you'd pound it out of roots or something," she said, standing on her toes to grab a can from behind the crushed pineapple. Before she came down, he did hug her, a hard arm around the waist. She dropped to her heels and leaned against his shoulder a minute. "You have this bad habit of turning up at the right times," she told him.

"Old Navajo custom—I'm hungry." He let her go. "What, just this dinky little can? Oh well, I'll put in chili sauce. I saw some of that."

"Chili sauce!"

"I thought you were fixing the salad."

The spaghetti was delicious and the salad almost crisp, but Shannon felt full quickly. Happy, that's what she was, she decided, really happy just listening to Stan's slow voice, watching his dark hands wind the spaghetti, not worrying about anything.

But he couldn't leave it alone. "Sorry you didn't go with your friends?" he asked, pushing his plate back at last. She shook her head.

"Nope. The spaghetti's too good." She lifted a strand from the tablecloth and popped it in her mouth.

"You didn't eat much—made me eat three-fourths of the bowl."

"It still was good."

"You haven't mentioned the company."

"Oh. Well, that too."

They smiled at each other, eyes holding. Such eye contact for Navajos, she knew, was an intimacy, a kind of long-distance embrace, but his look now wouldn't be considered casual even if his eyes were blue or hazel. Almost black, they burned.

She glanced away. "Maybe I ought to call Marci and tell her I'm here." He didn't answer. "Of course, she'll be furious if I bring her back without letting her spend the night," she told her yellow placemat awkwardly.

"Let her know she can come back if she wants to," Stan suggested. "Does she get homesick?"

"Not usually, but this is the first time she's been away from me since — since I left Don. We've become pretty attached."

"Call her up while I clear the table."

"I'm impressed." She moved away.

Marci was entirely disinterested in the fact that Shannon was at home. "I've got to go, Mom," she insisted. Shannon hung up feeling a quirk of loss. Every time she took Marci's hand now-adays, she wondered if it would be the last. Marci was ten. Surely eleven would be too old.

She joined Stan on the couch in front of the television, as usual, but their interest in the program was slight. Finally they ignored the television and talked, his arm along the sofa back, encircling her. Then there wasn't much to say, and she found herself moving closer, loving the look of her arm next to his, and the touch. Some halo of disbelief clung, reminding her he was big, he was Indian, he wasn't anything like Don — and they were both married, still, to people like themselves. But she couldn't draw back. Finally she said, "May I ask you one very Anglo question?"

"What is it?" He pulled away to look down into her face and she hesitated, afraid he wouldn't answer. But she couldn't continue with only the warmth in his eyes and arm. She had to have something in words that she could save to fight back her self doubts when he wasn't around. "How would you describe our relationship?"

He looked at her a minute. "We're friends," he said seriously, his arm tightening. "Good friends. We borrow from each other what we need."

Then he kissed her. Seconds later her hands found his hair, soft and thick. When the kiss ended, they were both smiling. He made a sound then, pulling her in, an expression of desire and release that flared inside her like joy. They kissed again and again; her fingers touched his face, ran along his shoulders, his arms. Minutes passed before he unlocked his arms enough to move his hands over her body. She fit into his hands, against him, pulling him down over her, trembling, finally, as he swung her legs out from the couch and lifted her. She couldn't remember ever wanting anyone so much.

Much later, half-waking next to him in her bed, it occurred to her how well-steeped Stan was in his people's stories of First Woman and First Man. Placing a hand flat on his warm back, she slept again. At dawn, he woke her slowly, bringing her from sleep to love almost without transition. When the room was light, he led her outside to show her coyote tracks all around the yard and underneath her bedroom window.

The next Saturday, Stan brought his finished yucca extract back and washed Marci's and Shannon's hair, then dressed both damp heads in Navajo knots tied with white cotton. Between last Saturday and this, the week had sped by. To Shannon's surprise, Stan had been right—they were friends. They chatted in the halls at school, watched Marci's favorite programs Wednesday evening, and walked home from the store together Thursday. She ignored Betsy's raised eyebrows but was glad to skip the excuses not to go out with the crowd the next weekend. No compulsion pushed her back into bed with Stan, though it seemed happily inevitable; but every time their eyes met, Shannon was warmed.

In fact, in her mellow state she found herself thinking more kindly of Don. Maybe he really did miss Marci. Maybe losing Heidi had been hard for him, though she wasn't ready to spare much sympathy on that. Still, quite ironically considering Monument Valley's new attractions, she was thinking more seriously about home. Of course, her mother had called twice to persuade her into committing her presence and Marci's at Thanksgiving dinner. If they stayed here, would they end up with Betsy and Dick ordering turkey dinner in Mexican Hat? No. Probably the two of them would split a chicken here in the compound together. But Marci would miss seeing her cousins and grandparents, as well as her father. Was that fair to her? Besides, Shannon knew that Stan would take the long drive to Navajo Mountain.

"All right," she had told Don Saturday morning when he called again. "We're coming. We'll go to Mom's for dinner, and then you can have Marci for the weekend. Sunday, by two or three, we'd better be on the road, earlier if it snows."

"That's great," Don said softly. "Thanks. You can't imagine how much I miss her. I miss you, too."

Her throat closed. "You don't have to say that."

"It's true. Let's find some time to talk while you're in town. Promise?"

Why did he do this? "I don't know, Don. I don't want to go through it all again." Damn him. Couldn't anything break their continuity, the inertia that drew them onward together? She wanted another walk.

A pause. "Shannon, I have to ask you something else. You don't make these conversations very easy. Would you please consider leaving Marci here until after the Christmas holidays? My caseload is light now and I could spend a lot of time with her. You'd be here during Christmas vacation and then—if you go back—you could take her then to finish the school year."

Shannon gasped. No wonder he was being so friendly. "That's more than a month, Don!"

"Yes, but you'd be here part of the time. A month isn't much in terms of shared custody, Shannon. You've got to be realistic."

"We don't have shared custody," she said tightly, knowing it was a feeble statement. He was a lawyer.

"That's right. And she's mine, too. When we broke up, you just took Marci and ran." '

"She was all I had!" She still is, she was going to add, but stopped. Why was she still so vulnerable just when she thought every wound had healed and sealed?

"I know, babe. But still, it was your decision to move her away, out of my reach."

"You were busy!" Shannon said meanly. "That was your decision."

"Shannon, please. Please understand. She's my child. I haven't seen her for months. I lost one of my children and I don't want to lose the other."

There was no answer to that, and after a few minutes of silence he apologized, but she was still reeling from the blow. "Don't cry, honey," he said, and she hated him for knowing she was sobbing into her fist. "Don't cry. Just think about it."

"Okay," she choked. "Good-bye."

The Navajo knot looked lovely, she saw in the mirror, but having her hair pulled back emphasized her still-reddened eyes. Marci skipped off to show Angela her hair and returned with news. "Angela's grandma saw a skinwalker outside her hogan," she reported.

"She saw the skinwalker?" Stan asked.

"She heard it and then she went outside and found big tracks. The skinwalker rattled her stovepipe and chased her sheep around. That's how she knew it was outside."

"I caught Jeanette telling a skinwalker story at school yesterday," Shannon told Stan. "Something must be going around."

"Angie and I are both drawing pictures of it tonight," Marci said. "We'll compare them in the morning. Maybe Jim will drive us out to the Yeibechai rocks to give them to her grandma."

"Okay. Take your crayons to bed with you — just keep them up on the nightstand off the sheets. I'll turn off your light in a while." Marci looked carefully out the windows before leaving the room.

"Want a walk?" Shannon asked Stan after tucking in Marci for the third time.

"If you do. It's cold."

"I know. And I'm kind of achy. Maybe we'd better not."

"Once she's asleep we can go over to my place. We'd better not leave her awake with skinwalkers around."

"You're right." She sat down beside him, subdued, picked up his long hand in both of hers. His other hand rubbed her back in slow circles. "Talk," he said.

She shrugged. "Don wants to keep Marci from Thanksgiving until after Christmas."

He nodded. Stated like that, it didn't sound unreasonable.

"I guess that's not so bad but I just . . . don't want to leave her. I suppose I'll go home for Christmas, so we'd be together for two weeks then anyway."

He nodded again with a sound she realized Navajos make in conversation together, a yes, go on, I understand, sort of grunt. She'd never heard it in a conversation in English. She lifted his hand and kissed it.

"Oh, it's not that simple," she admitted, rubbing his hand along her cheek. She let his hand drop, talking faster. "It's something Don said. Marci had a brother who died in his sleep when he was three months old. Crib death." She wiped with both hands at predictable tears.

Stan reached for a box of tissues, giving her time. "The same with my brother's baby," he said. "It happens sometimes."

"He blames me," she gasped, mopping up. More tears flowed.

Stan waited until she blew her nose. "If it happened down here, you could say the baby was witched. You could seek revenge and go to a medicine man."

"Do you believe that?"

"Superstition, mainly. But no more superstitious than what you're saying." He took her wet face in his hands. "He doesn't blame you. I don't believe it. No one you would marry could blame you."

She broke away and went for a drink of water, tried to stop crying, then returned. "You're right. I guess I blame me. I've always felt that I should have noticed something, should have heard something, should have checked the baby sooner. Maybe it's irrational but I never could make it up to Don for losing his son."

Stan nodded, pulled her down beside him.

She picked up his hands again. "So when he fell in love with Heidi," she went on determinedly, "I knew it was only compensation, paying me back for his loss. I couldn't keep Steven, I couldn't keep Don. So I decided to keep Marci."

They sat quietly, holding each other, then Stan leaned away. "Maybe he couldn't make it up to you," he said. "You bore the baby. How would he feel watching you go through all that, then seeing your heart break?"

"I don't know. I can't remember. I guess he tried to reach me."

"One thing about men," Stan said so sadly that Shannon wondered what lay under his words, "we don't like to feel helpless."

She thought about that. "And he was helpless. He lost Steven, then me, then Marci, now Heidi." She took a long breath and tried to shift the subject slightly. "What was your nephew's name?"

Stan shook his head and shrugged.

"Oh. I forgot," she said. "Navajos don't speak of the dead. I'm sorry, but Ste—my baby was too little to have a chindi, wasn't he? How could he give anyone ghost sickness?"

He smiled. "I think there's more to the custom than that, Shannon. Navajos have lost so many babies, so many dear ones over the years. Fear of ghost sickness protected us from small-pox and plague, but it also makes us pay attention to the living. And we have ceremonies. We bless the sun in the morning, we blow pollen, we praise the rain."

"But what do you do with your grief?" After all, she coped. She seldom talked about Steven, she supported Marci, she went on living.

"You wear it out," he said levelly. "You wear it until you wear it out." A flashback hit Shannon then, a vision of her grandmother, a small suitcase in hand, boarding a city bus for the Salt Lake Temple to do work for the dead. Her parents did the same now that they were retired, except they drove their Mercedes. Shannon had always considered work for the dead a colossal waste of time when there was so much to do for the living. But maybe that was their attraction to that ceremony, the sacred repetition of ritual that wore out their grief, connected them to their dead parents and siblings, to Steven. Families had so many people to lose. She and Don had married in the temple, and never returned, but her walks at sunset—what happened between her and the sky, the stones, and the land was becoming a kind of ritual.

Her eyes felt as weary as they did swollen. She must look terrible. "I guess you're going to Navajo Mountain for Christmas, aren't you?"

"I am." He folded her into his arms and kissed her, then held her for a long minute. "And right now you're going to bed."

He walked with her down the hall, turned off Marci's light. "I'll switch off lights on my way out," he said. "I did a great job on your hair."

Monday, the Monday before Thanksgiving, Shannon assigned her students an essay on skinwalkers. Their pencils scratched the theme paper busily. She stared out the window at the blue desert sky. November had turned as bright as August, but not as warm. One day snow would come. She liked the look of snow on the red rocks, and it didn't stay on the roads long. After class, a dozen students stayed behind to tell her their stories, their eyes wide, their hands gesturing. They reminded her of crouching on the church steps with other MIA Maids sharing stories about the Three Nephites and evil spirits, scaring each other spitless.

In faculty meeting, the principal discussed the holiday schedule. "Every year," he said, "we have faculty members who don't return for the second semester. Please, for the sake of your students, if any of you have an inkling that you won't be back after the holidays, let me know."

Shannon felt Stan's eyes on her. She didn't move.

That night she corrected the skinwalker essays while Marci brushed her teeth, read, fell asleep. They were the best papers yet. Probably she was learning what to assign as much as they were learning how to write. She remembered how Ben's eyes had flashed describing the skinwalker racing his friend's car out of a canyon, how shy Alice had edged against her as she whispered her tale. Her uncle had actually captured a skinwalker, stringing it up, but it turned into a coyote at the last moment, she said. On her drive to Salt Lake City, Shannon predicted, their stories and faces would speak in her thoughts.

After Marci fell asleep, Shannon walked outside to see the stones and stars, then went next door to Stan. They made love gently at first, beginning already to miss each other, then fiercely, celebrating their union. Afterwards, still entangled, Stan told her he had a job offer from the Bureau of Indian Affairs elementary school at Navajo Mountain. If he took the offer, it would mean teaching physical education instead of coaching football and would pay a lot less. They would want his decision by the Christmas break.

"Between Thanksgiving and Christmas we can both make decisions," Shannon said, wanting only to relish the peace and comfort of the night.

She stayed awake a long time after Stan slept, watching the moonlight, broken into panes by the window, move across their bodies. She recalled how Stan had defended Don the other night even while holding her, Don's wife, in his arms — and by defending Don had shielded her from Don's perceived blame. Some of her guilt was gone, she realized. She considered whether Heidi, once her friend, had ever taken her part with Don. Most likely she had, a woman in Don's arms who, through him, sensed Shannon's grief. Once that surprising conclusion settled like certainty in her solar plexus, Shannon imagined Don and Heidi together, as she and Stan were now, and for the first time felt no pain. If Don had found solace even temporarily — a possibility that had struck her as terribly unfair at the time — she could almost be happy someone had given him what she could not. Not then.

Tuesday night, Stan took Shannon and Marci to Kayenta for dinner. Marci bubbled with excitement about staying with her father for three weeks until Shannon joined them for Christmas. Shannon tried to hide her chagrin at herself, for somehow she had assumed that Marci didn't miss Don much.

Wednesday morning, Shannon packed her car and Stan loaded his. "Good weather for a journey," he commented, rearranging Marci's menagerie of stuffed animals and closing the back door.

Shannon smiled up at him. "Yes. I'll see you Sunday night."

"Sunday night." He picked up Marci for a hug. "Maybe I'll see you in the new year."

"Definitely," Marci chimed. Definitely was Marci's favorite word now, and Stan chuckled. "Meanwhile, send me a picture of your boys at Navajo Mountain," she instructed.

"Okay." Stan put Marci in the front seat, fastened her seat belt, and walked Shannon around the car. Since they were outside the compound, he wouldn't kiss her. Practically everyone in Monument Valley had relatives at Navajo Mountain. He held her in his eyes. "You're not afraid to drive back alone?"

"I'll have a lighter load without all those stuffed animals," she shrugged, but his eyes didn't smile. "I won't feel alone when I'm coming back," she told him.

He waved as long as she could see him in the rear view mirror, until she turned north up the highway, watching for livestock and creatures, confident that they could all share the unfenced road.

HE CALLED US
MORMON NUNS

AS JANEECE HANDED A STEAMING BOWL OF BROCCOLI
to Maggie across the table, I told them what Gary
Gilchrist had said. "He called us Mormon nuns."

I watched as Janeece tipped her head in that quizzical way
that won't wrinkle the neck at age thirty-six. Maggie took the
broccoli, which was tipping too, then drolly rolled her eyes.

"Let me get this straight," she said. Janeece lifted her eyes
to mine, anticipating a punchline. Maggie spaced her words.
"Gary Gilchrist called us Mormon nuns."

I nodded and took my turn at the broccoli. Maggie had
overcooked it a little. She's casual about limp vegetables, and
Janeece is a fanatic for crisp-tender.

Actually, I'd generously included myself in Gary's assess-
ment. He had called *them* Mormon nuns that day in our department store lunchroom. He works in design. I'm buyer for in-
fants and children. Of course I didn't tell my roommates the
guilty truth — that (in the context of the conversation) I'd agreed
with him.

Maggie passed the mushrooms Janeece had sauteed.

"Hmmm," she mused, giving it time. "He's rather a nun himself, isn't he?"

We laughed. "Rather," I said.

Now Maggie had her teeth deep in trout. "Somehow I don't think nuns eat this well," she muttered around it, dabbing her chin with a paper napkin.

"And I never promised to be poor!" Janeece added.

"You didn't? But you both work for the church!"

They giggled, although Janeece tucked her chin down, meaning I was a trifle worldly.

"Touché," Maggie picked it up. "They should have sworn us to poverty the same way they swear you to chastity in the temple."

"Oh, well," Janeece demurred, her color rising attractively. "To chastity, but not to celibacy."

"Haven't noticed much difference," Maggie said, "have you?"

I laughed with them, savoring my trout. Dinner was the high point of the day. I skipped breakfast or jogged at lunch to offset the calories I'd consume later.

Taking Maggie and then Janeece as roommates made a perfect setup, although my salary was a little higher than theirs, and my position implied more responsibility. Even with a history degree, Maggie could work in the genealogy department for years without rising in rank. Janeece knew the temple nursery had no room for advancement. I had the additional advantage of being able to cuss out management, something they couldn't do with a clear conscience.

So I made the house payments, and they appreciated my worldly job that made them feel closer to the spiritual center. Sometimes I cussed with extra vigor to improve everyone's mental health, even at risk of my immortal soul.

Only the week before, I'd given us all an evening's catharsis after I spent the day breaking in a new boss with only half my experience. Until that morning he'd been the boys' wear buyer.

Debacles like that led Gary Gilchrist and me to meet weekly in the cafeteria for mini-purges of the job's frustrations. Gary was tall and pale with such light red hair it looked pink. Matching freckles spotted his nose and cheeks. Gary was single, never-married—just as we were. Being a man, he bore more guilt. We, poor things, were simply unchosen. So he scourged his culpability with a clever, acidic tongue.

He loved hearing about my life in my little house near town, although he'd never met Maggie or Janeece. That day I told him how my boss-cussing did them good.

"But let me get this straight," he said, smearing his hair back in the anxious gesture that belied his superior smile. "Your roommates work for the church five days a week, then spend Sundays there too? That's incredible."

"Their whole lives revolve around the church," I said.

He shook his head and I stifled a smile.

"You know what they are?" he asked. "They're nuns. Mormon nuns. Married to the church."

We laughed. "Well, but they don't wear wedding rings," I reminded.

"All the worse!" He smiled at the waitress who dallied nearby. "The church should give them wedding rings, gold ones. What are they—kept women?"

That's the part I didn't tell my roommates. I wasn't sure they would laugh.

I remember that evening clearly, how Maggie stood after dinner, brushing crumbs from her favorite smock. Then she methodically stacked the dishes. Janeece tossed her curls before the bathroom mirror adjoining the kitchen, checking to see if it was time for another rinse. Her voice implored us.

"Really, would you mind terribly listening to the new part of my Tupperware presentation?"

Maggie rolled her eyes at me, her hands full of dishes. The doorbell saved us answering.

"We paid the paper carrier," Maggie said, holding out the plates for the silverware in my hands, "so it must be the home teachers. Would you get it, Carolyn?"

I stepped over Janeece's sandals in the living room doorway. Each was made from nine slender straps. On my way to the door I thought how Maggie's orange and brown outfit and Janeece's pale yellow frock typified September, an uncertain month. Janeece lingered in summer, but Maggie was comfortably into fall.

Since I answered the door, naturally I saw Lou Maher first. That seemed an important point later on. He stood beside Brother Walsh, who usually brought his wife along. Brother Walsh told me Lou was new in the ward and would be his junior home teaching companion. I noted his tall, sturdy frame, the dark red hair, heavy brows and intent brown eyes. When he shook my hand, I spied a fading, white circle around the root of his ring finger.

They came in and sat down. Maggie shook their hands, then hustled to the kitchen for lemonade. Janeece trailed in behind her on the second trip, still shoeless. She perched on the arm of Maggie's armchair, tentative as a thirteen-year-old. But she smiled at them blazingly, and it's her thousand-watt smile that wins her the chair at the guest book at friends' wedding receptions. It dazzles away her thin, slightly lame leg, the result of polio.

We learned quickly that Lou's wife had died eight months earlier from a tubal pregnancy. They had no children. He was a counselor in the church's social service department. Since Brother Walsh was a guide on Welfare Square, it turned out I was the only one who didn't work for the church. We laughed about that.

"Ah, a pretty girl like you working in the big, wicked world," Brother Walsh teased.

"What an exaggeration," I told him. I met Lou's eyes and thought they snapped with interest. But I'd met too many Lous to be overwhelmed. I glanced at Janeece. The light from the western windows lit her sideways, pinking her cheeks, accenting the delicacy of her bones, her small head. She was at her most Dresden.

Probably I sighed. I am perfectly ordinary, average height and weight, medium-length brown hair, hazel eyes. I look like everybody's cousin. Maggie, with her comfortable cap of glossy, dark hair and her tortoise-shell glasses has more presence.

The men stood, preparing to leave, while Brother Walsh teased Janeece about all "her kids" in the temple nursery. That's when Lou shook my hand and asked my advice on what to buy his nephew for his third birthday. Then, still holding my hand in his warm, fleshy one, he drew me onto the front porch. When I stopped rambling about overalls and jackets, he said, "I really appreciate your advice. I'm just beginning to get out and around now. Would you like to go to a movie sometime?"

Behind me Janeece's laughter tinkled, and I nearly glanced back to see if he was asking her. But his eyes were on my face. I told him yes.

"Well, how about Friday? Maybe at 7:30?"

"Fine," I said as the others joined us on the porch.

He squeezed my hand, let it go, and gave me what can only be described as a meaningful glance. I smiled at him, then followed the others inside to face the music.

Maggie was back in the chair. She took one look at my face and burst out laughing. "Don't look so surprised! I told you that turquoise blouse brings out the green in your eyes."

"I am surprised." I lifted my voice to carry into the kitchen where it sounded as if Janeece might be sorting Tupperware. She'd started the dishwasher, too.

"So — where are you going?" Maggie asked.

"A movie. On Friday. Oh no. What if he likes westerns?"

"So you'll go a western. I'd bet on a family comedy. Very strategic."

I said nothing.

"Here," she urged, "have a chocolate and share my guilt."

There was still no voice from the kitchen. I sighed. Janeece must be mad, hurt, jealous, and would never say it.

Maggie looked at me almost as meaningfully as Lou had. "Janeece," she called casually, "come get a chocolate. Bring your Tupperware, and we'll listen to your spiel."

Silence. Then Janeece walked in, balancing a white plastic butter dish on the palm of one hand. "It's about this butter dish. I wonder about using the same little anecdote the district seller used."

"What's that?" I virtuously compelled my interest.

"It goes like this. You show them the butter dish, how the lid seals, all that." Her thin hands flew as she demonstrated. "Then you say: 'And another thing: If your kiddies have hamsters or goldfish or white mice or even parakeets around. . . . Well, you know what becomes of little pets like that! And if and when you need it, this butter dish does beautifully as a tiny coffin.' "

Maggie and I lasted until our startled eyes met. Then we burst into wailing, uncontrollable laughter. I know Janeece smiled. I saw her when I pried my eyes open and gasped for air. Maggie's face was crimson.

"I just thought," Janeece said defensively. "I mean I couldn't tell—I thought for people who have children . . . "

But her voice squeaked on "children" and she took the butter dish and fled.

Still weak from laughter, Maggie and I fortified ourselves with another chocolate each, locked the door, pulled the blinds, patted one another's back as we choked down chocolate, still laughing, and went to our separate rooms.

That Friday evening Janeece left for her Tupperware party

before Lou picked me up for our date. I was glad. I'd absorbed enough tension already, and hoped Lou would be as easygoing as he seemed.

I remember watching his square hands on the steering wheel as we drove away. He talked as he drove, recounting his day for me: the morning meeting, the couple with a rebellious adolescent at two, an adopted child looking for her natural parents at four. I wondered if this had been his pattern during his marriage, to relate the day's story each evening. Then I wondered if his wife had worked. I asked. He looked startled.

"Oh, no. I mean, she was a bank clerk before we married, but there was no reason for her to work afterward." He leaned toward me a little. "I'm not a rich man, Carolyn, but I'll always support my family."

"I see. Well."

If we married, just if, would he want me to recount my day? I'd tell him about reordering a whole line of fluffy rompers or lining up the logistics for a buying trip to New York. Had I mentioned those buying trips to him?

I looked up to find him watching me intently. "We forgot something," he said.

"We did? What?"

"Well, not forgot exactly, but neglected."

We were at a stop sign on 500 South. There was nowhere to turn around "Well, is it important?"

"I think so. Carolyn, would you say a word of prayer and ask the Lord's spirit to be with us this evening?"

"Oh, well, sure." I waited for him to cross the intersection and park, perhaps under a tree with long, still-leafy limbs. But I saw that he sat behind the wheel with his eyes intently closed. Obviously he felt some urgency.

I glanced into the rear-view mirror, then bowed my head and said a few swift phrases, sure the Lord would understand that a green sedan was approaching us from the rear. As we crossed the intersection, I wondered how we'd been seen from behind — maybe we seemed to have dropped something? I could hardly wait to tell Maggie.

But it was Janeece's voice, not Maggie's, that I imagined in my ear, as clearly as if she'd climbed into the back seat. Or, rather, as if she, not I, were with him.

"Would you believe," she said, her voice tinged with wonder, "he asked me to pray at a stop sign? Just as if the Lord's so close . . ."

"Maybe in the green sedan," I imagined Maggie interjecting, and I smiled. Lou, of course, was left out of all this, so I said to him. "I'm so glad I got back from New York in time to see the leaves turn on the mountains. I've always loved our autumns."

That won me a warm glance that grew puzzled. "Do you have family in New York?"

We were pulling into Trolley Square. "Oh, no. Business. New York is where we generally order the clothes for the department. Sometimes Los Angeles or Chicago, but usually New York."

He was quiet, winding between the narrow parking lots. He waited for a red Volkswagen to pull out. With the car parked, Lou looked at me.

"Carolyn, you're a very attractive woman for your age. I hate to think of you in a place like New York." Then he patted my hand. "It's not your fault, of course."

As we walked to the theater I wondered what wasn't my fault — my job or my attractiveness — for my age. Then, as my heels teetered on the uneven cobble stones, Lou took my arm just above the elbow with the same confidence with which he turned the steering wheel. His hand was so warm, my arm so encompassed, that I decided to relax for the rest of the evening.

Maggie was right about the movie. It was a domestic comedy with wide-eyed children, a curvy, confused mother, and a knowing-best husband. Lou loved it.

So did Janeece. I heard her in my ear all the way through. She was charmed by the way Lou wiped his eyes when the exhausted mother covered up the rotten little boy who'd fallen asleep on the floor of his closet. Lou's chuckle at the mother's frustrations and his concern when the family's problems seemed insurmountable (music rising), struck Janeece as unusually sensitive.

Walking across the square for Chinese-American food, I decided I was becoming jaded—and I was tired of monitoring everyone's feelings. Obviously I'd been single too long and knew my roommates too well. Until I smelled the soup, I wasn't even hungry. But over the soup, Lou led our movie chatter toward our own lives. Mine in particular.

"I know you must hear this often," Lou said, (and I barely kept myself from chanting the question with him), "but why hasn't a girl like you ever married?" Whatever he saw in my face made him twinkle at me, "I'll bet you've broken some hearts!"

I smiled. "Well, the situation has never looked right, Lou."

He nodded understandingly. "But marriage does appeal to you, doesn't it?" he probed.

"Some marriages do. Some don't. Grandma used to say that it takes a mighty good husband to be better than none at all. I guess I look around and think she's probably right."

His eyes widened, then he laughed. "Well, that's the truth. I certainly see that in my career."

Our shrimp came then, and for a while, we ate without talking.

"So . . . ," he said and smiled meaningfully into my eyes. His dark eyes were adding, subtracting, totalling me, and his fingers pointed, touching lightly, above his plate. "So maybe you weren't so surprised to end up a career woman?"

I shrugged. "I didn't anticipate it. It just happened."

He tried again. "Carolyn, about this job of yours. Do you feel it's what the Lord intends you to do, or is it just a useful way to support yourself?"

"I don't know, it's not a bad job."

He frowned. "Well, haven't you had some guidance on the issue? Your patriarchal blessing, for instance?"

I couldn't help chuckling. "I don't think it took very well."

"What do you mean?"

"First it said I would have a large and faithful family. Then it told me to get an education in the science of fabrics so I could clothe my family in modesty."

He nodded. "And?"

"Well, Lou, I don't have a family and I absolutely cannot sew. I've tried. It makes me itch. It makes my skin crawl."

There was a pause. He pushed his plate aside and folded his hands on the table. Suddenly I wondered when I'd made this appointment with a counselor.

"What about this?" he asked, his voice slowing, dropping intimately. "What if it turns out that you do have a family, a large and faithful one, that you clothe in modesty. Maybe it's just a matter of timing."

His eyes stayed on my face, warm, inviting, even a little humorous. His warmth surged across the formica and felt good. I couldn't help smiling at him any more than the mother in the movie could help collapsing into her handsome husband's arms.

"Oh, I'd clothe them, Lou. But it would be off the racks. One thing I know, is how to buy good clothes, often on sale."

He nodded as if I'd come close enough and motioned for the check.

"He's so understanding," Janeece whispered, as we went out the door into the September night.

It wasn't just the story Lou told me on the way home that

decided the outcome of our relationship. But it's the first thing I think of now that he's married and I'm not.

He parked the car a little way from my house and stretched his arm along the back of the seat. I turned, moving closer without actually sliding over. I wondered if there would be a closing prayer, too, although the finger he ran down the shins of my crossed legs didn't seem to indicate one.

After gazing at me a minute, Lou grinned broadly.

"What is it?"

He chuckled. "Oh, just something that popped into my head. I'm not sure I should tell you."

I didn't urge him, but he continued. "You see, I'd been counseling a young man we'll call Jay for several months. He was a returned missionary who'd had some problems." Lou snickered again, warming to his story. His hand had found my right shoulder. He rubbed it. His voice was low and warm. "So Jay called me one morning all upset. He'd had an interview with his bishop the night before."

"MmmHMM," I said, glad we were so lighthearted.

"And the bishop had asked him a very disturbing question."

"What else is new?" I asked flippantly, tilting my eyes up at him. His hand rubbing my shoulder stopped, then started again, pressing harder. "Well, you know, Carolyn, bishops are some of the church's best men, and they have the hardest jobs. They just don't have the experience and training that a professional does."

I nodded and let it go.

"Well, what his bishop asked him was this." His hand wandered down my arm, then back up quickly. "He asked Jay if he'd ever behaved illicitly with a dead deer."

"If he'd what?" But Lou had burst out laughing. "You're kidding," I insisted when he stopped for breath.

"No. And of course Jay was terribly upset. So he called me and asked if that was an appropriate question. Of course it wasn't, but Jay was upset and I admit I was curious, so I got his bishop's name and called him."

"What did he say?"

He chuckled again. "Well, fortunately Jay was one of the first few he'd asked that question. You see, another young man had come in not long before, and poured out a long confession. At the height of his degradation, this guy had been hunting (and drinking a little, I suspect) and he shot a doe. After he cut her throat, he was suddenly seized by this strange obsession and . . . " He shrugged and licked his lips.

"I see."

"Anyway, the bishop was so shaken by the confession that he began asking other young men."

In the pause that followed, I waited for Janeece's comment in my ear. I knew why she was silent. Lou wouldn't have told her that story. Now he was leaning forward to kiss me. I don't remember the kiss, really. In my head was this scene of a yellowed hillside and a deer slowly dying.

I do remember how he cupped my chin after the kiss. I looked back into his eyes, wondering. "Carolyn," he whispered, and smiled. "In the world but not of it." He kissed the tip of my nose so tenderly tears sprang to my eyes. Lou unwound his arm, removed his knee from against mine and got out of the car. As he came around to my door, I saw him mop the back of his neck.

I didn't say much about the date, which made my roommates suspicious I was falling in love. I remember Saturday as a pale, tense day. I felt the tension, Janeece showed it, and Maggie ignored it.

I had every right to fall in love with Lou Maher, to marry him and have children and quit my job. Hadn't I always wanted to? I even had the right to tell Maggie and Janeece they'd have to move out because Lou was moving in. (Although I suspected he'd want me to sell my house and move into his, or buy one together.) Why shouldn't I want babies to fill the rompers on the racks and a warm pair of arms greeting me at the end of the day?

So why was I depressed?

Lou sat by me at sacrament meeting on Sunday, and I invited him to come over for homemade peach ice cream that evening. I let him hold my hand during the second speaker, but during the closing song I made up my mind. I was going to throw him like a bouquet into Janeece's waiting hands. When heads bowed, he squeezed my knee, and I wondered how to do it.

At dinner that afternoon I took a risk. We'd roasted a small turkey, garnished it with cranberry-orange sauce, and sacrificed potatoes for Janeece's mushroom dressing. A breeze wandered through the open windows. By the end of the meal we were all relaxed again. It felt like heaven.

"You've got to help me," I said.

They looked at me expectantly.

"It's Lou." Janeece looked down at her plate. Maggie's eyes didn't budge from mine.

"He's a great guy, and I'd hate to hurt his feelings, but—" Janeece looked up. Now I had to be careful.

"Don't tell me there's something wrong with him," she said, as if I'd tossed hundreds of sleek, silvery salmon back into the stream.

"Oh, no. He seems very nice, very warm. That's why I'm so depressed. I can't figure out why, but it's not going to work out between us. I just know it's not, and it seems unfair to waste his time."

"He does seem eager to get the show on the road," Maggie said.

"Well, his wife's been gone eight months," Janeece put in. "He must be dreadfully lonely."

I sighed. "That's it. So anyway, I think I'm going to get called into work to do inventory tonight. After we make ice cream, of course. Maybe when its nearly ready to eat."

They thought about my idea. They smiled. Janeece's smile rivaled the afternoon sun collecting in the sheer curtains that halfway circle the table.

"Don't worry about a thing," Maggie said.

"You two stay put," Janeece offered. "I'll clear up." She rose, light as a dandelion's white blur, and began gathering silverware.

Maggie was staring at me with calculating eyes. I returned her look. She lifted her goblet as if to make a toast. "You could get Gary Gilchrist to call you this evening about the inventory."

I nodded. "Good idea."

"He called us Mormon nuns," Janeece reminded, drifting back to the table for more dishes. Her voice lilted.

Maggie and I smiled across the table. "What does he know?" she said.

"I've been thinking there's another word for it," I told them. Janeece paused, head up, bending to lift the turkey platter as Maggie snitched a final morsel.

"Sisters," I said. Then we laughed at how a chilly gust furled the curtains around us like a sudden veil.

SUSANNA IN THE
MEADOW

TWELVE YEARS AFTER SUSANNA MARRIED FINN, SHE considered the fact that he always changed her name. Almost immediately upon dating him she'd become Susy, a romantic endearment, she thought, though she'd trained her classmates from kindergarten to her junior year in college to say Susanna. Occasionally, in a hurry, a friend said Sue.

But then when she and Finn married four days after graduation, Finn had edged into Susan or Susanne, though he never abandoned Susy. Really, when she thought about it, the only time he called her Susanna was when he was being silly. "Oh, Susanna!" he'd sing from the shower, glass door ajar so she could hear, "oh don't you hurry me." Or at Christmas time, "SuSANna! SuSANna! Hallelujah! Hallelujah!"

Sitting cross-legged in one of Finn's white shirts and her favorite jeans, she stared out the picture window and meditated on this. (Finn called it daydreaming.) Probably she'd never have had this insight at all, except for last night's dream. In the dream she'd been sitting in a sidewalk cafe somewhere, Paris, she hoped, and heard a familiar voice calling, "Su-sy. Su-sannn." She was trying to talk with someone across the table, Violet maybe, and the voice kept interrupting her thoughts.

"Why doesn't that woman answer or that stupid man shut up!" she finally blurted in the dream.

Violet — it had been Violet — smiled mysteriously the way she so often did at dream group. "Maybe he's calling you."

Susanna had flipped her napkin over her lap. "You know that's not my name," she said and woke up.

Susanna closed her eyes and rolled her head slowly all the way around, trying to ease the tension in her neck. "YOU know that's not my name." Had there been a little emphasis on the "you"?

She sighed. She could bring up the dream when they got together next Wednesday. "Do you feel he's trying to diminish you? To abridge you?" Mimi would ask, pale hair fluttering about her head like feathers as she talked.

"Or close me off," she heard her own voice reply. "Susanna is so open. It sort of fades off into the distance. Susy. Susan. Susanne. They have boundaries. Perimeters."

"Safe," she heard Violet say.

A short red figure appeared through the window, trudging so single-mindedly that Susanna had to smile. Molly looked like an elf in that parka when she wore her red corduroy pants. Only a few blond wisps poking from the hood broke the scarlet. She moved from concrete square to square like a little red game piece. Susanna wondered what was in her daughter's head. Susanna stretched her legs and arms, then hopped up to tiptoe to the front door, feeling the pull in her calf muscles.

She came down on her heels as she opened it.

"Hello, Muffin. Have a hug?" Susanna called out. Molly's cold face cooled hers. "Mmmm. How was school today?"

"Okay," Molly said, as she always did. She wouldn't open up until her coat was off and she was perched on the counter, snacking while Susanna drifted around the kitchen conjuring up dinner.

"Josh has soccer practice and Kerry is still asleep, so it looks like we're alone . . . together."

Molly looked up gravely at her conspiratorial tone. "That doesn't often happen," she said. "Have you had a productive day?"

"Rather. How about you?"

There was a muffled sound of chewing. Molly loved oatmeal cookies if they had chocolate chips instead of raisins, and oatmeal upset Susanna's stomach. She made them often. The kids were happy, and she could leave them alone.

"I finished a whole section of my thesis, once and for all!" Susanna reported. "And I took Kerry and went to the grocery store and cleaned up the house, specializing in three overhead cupboards. How's that."

Molly nodded. "I'm glad you won't be working on your thesis tonight. Maybe we can play Scrabble."

"How about Junior Scrabble. Then you don't have to figure numbers so much."

"I beg your pardon," Molly said, and Susanna stifled a chuckle. Did any other second graders talk like Molly? Susanna liked to think she had something to do with Molly's brightness, but, really, she was so much like her dad. You'd think that with only one daughter, she'd be a little more . . . well, winsome.

Still it was Molly who said that night at dinner, as she pounded the bottom of the catsup bottle with little effect, "Want to hear my dream? You can put it in your thesis."

Finn snorted but covered it with a smile.

Susanna leaned forward. "A dream from last night?"

"Oh, no," Finn said mildly, shaking his head. "Another dreamer in the family."

"You're a dreamer, too," Molly told him. "You just don't pay attention."

"I dreamed you bought me a Yamaha," Josh said. "I could drive it, too. Race it."

"That's one dream that will never come true," Finn exclaimed. "Do you know how many heads I've put back together on kids with Yamahas? Pass the squash, Susan. I've got a high council meeting in twenty minutes."

"One emergency after another," Susanna said lightly, and Finn grimaced, then grinned.

Being an emergency room physician wasn't the most lucrative position in the medical field, but its regular hours allowed Finn to be very active in church leadership.

"What does Josh's Yamaha mean, Mom?" Molly said.

"Well, a vehicle often means the energy in one's life," Susanna said. "If that were my dream, Josh, I guess I'd feel like my life was really moving along and I was directing it well. Did you have a good feeling in the dream?"

"Oh, yeah. It was great. I was tearing up this hill with sagebrush and stuff on it."

Finn gave Susanna a dark look. "Don't encourage him. No motorcycles in this family. I wish you could see just one kid with brain damage."

"That's not the point and you know it, Finn. It's a dream about his feelings. Not about getting a motorcycle."

"Why can't I get a motorcycle?" Josh complained. "I'd wear a helmet."

"Have dessert without me if there is some," Finn said. "I don't want to be late."

"How late will you be coming home?"

"Who knows? We've got one of each to hear tonight." He patted her shoulder as he swung by — just, she thought, the way he patted the mother of a patient.

"Each what?" Molly asked.

"Sinners," Josh said. "Don't you know anything?"

"I can't sin until I'm eight." Molly stuck out her tongue.

Susanna was in the bathtub, lights out, a candle burning in the corner, the froth of scented bubbles all around her. Kerry's asleep, Molly's asleep, Josh is in bed, she told herself, trying to relax all her muscles. She would summon up Lila tonight, to bring her closer to Finn. He might not like her dream group and her finding out all these new insights and powers within herself, but he liked Lila. And, Susanna smiled, so did she.

Oh, she had denied Lila's existence for a long time, even as a teenager, certainly as a bride, then as a young mother. She could remember lying in bed one Sunday night wondering if a pregnant primary president could or should ever be sexy. Most of the women in her dream group had trouble admitting they had a Lila in them somewhere, but, Susanna confessed, she had been rather eager to discover her. Someone, after all, let that top button slip open and her skirt creep above her knee. When Susanna noticed, she hurriedly adjusted her clothing, her eyes as innocent as dawn.

So when the group had a Halloween party that year, they'd done two madcap things. One, they insisted that everyone come as some unintegrated part of herself. Two, they invited their husbands.

Violet had come as Mabel, with eyes downcast to her Peter Pan collar, feet demurely crossed under a navy, pleated skirt. Her husband was very jovial, loud really, all evening. Mimi arrived in her husband's three-piece suit and hauling his briefcase. They'd looked alike, since he wore a suit, too. And Susanna had blushingly bought a black negligee at a shop she'd never gone to before, and borrowed Violet's embroidered slippers. The night of the party, she judiciously adjusted her underwear beneath the negligee and went as Lila.

Finn spent the evening tying the bow at her cleavage, but when they went home that night, he'd only been frustrated that she had so much on underneath.

Remembering that night, Susanna slid lower into the warm water. Hurry, she telegraphed to Finn, yet she didn't want to get out of the tub yet. She imagined him sitting around a long table, facing other men in their white shirts and ties. Some penitent would be sobbing down at the end. In the dream group, they lounged all over each other's living rooms. If someone wept, the nearest ones — it didn't matter who — reached out. I don't want to look at this, they were saying in real life, but they confronted whatever monster it was when they told the dream.

Now maybe Finn and the others were kneeling in prayer. Did they clap their hands down on each other's shoulders when they prayed as they did when they blessed a baby? She couldn't imagine them holding hands. But she had watched them walk from that meeting before and had seen how their straight-suited bodies brushed in passing, heard the harmonizing fifths in their voices. She felt a sudden sympathy for Finn and his meetings.

Was that the front door? She sat up, listened. No, but Finn would be coming soon. One last dip, then she pulled the plug and ran the soap through the bubbles a few times to hear them shatter.

She got out, smoothed oil over her skin, dried it off, bent and brushed her hair down from the nape, straightened and furled it back. Only then did she puff out the candle and turn on the overhead light. She reached for her peach nightgown and let it glide down over her flesh. She shivered and tinted her cheeks the same peach color.

She checked the children and went into the bedroom to light candles there and turn the radio to the all-night music station. She wished they could afford a stereo for the bedroom. She quelled her impatience for Finn's return by accepting this quiet time to meditate, and stretched out sensuously on the bedspread. But when Finn came into the room, she jumped and gasped.

"Sorry," he said. His voice sounded far away.

She stared at him.

"Didn't mean to wake you," he said. "Or be so late."

He hung his suit jacket in the closet and undid his belt.

"I was waiting. I guess I fell asleep."

She tried to recover her mood, but her body lay stiff as a fork in a satin case. What was wrong? He stepped into the bathroom and shut the door. When he came out, she was writing in her dream journal. She heard him sigh.

"I thought you only had to do that in the morning."

"Just this quick little dream I had, waiting for you." She closed the journal and smiled at him. "See, I'm through."

She let the shoulder of her nightgown slip down and shook out her hair, as he lay down with a stretch of bedspread between them.

He closed his eyes. "Rough night," he said without opening them.

"Oh. Well, would you like a massage? A warm shower, then a massage?" He didn't answer. Maybe he'd fallen asleep, too. She crossed her legs and opened her dream journal to read what she'd written. She felt his eyes on her and looked up.

"I get so damn tired listening to people's traumas, and you get into all this just for fun," he said.

"It's not just for fun. We discover a lot."

His mouth tightened and he nodded. "Yeah. So do we."

"What happened tonight? Did you . . . "

"We excommunicated two people, disfellowshipped one. Adultery, homosexuality, and heresy. I gave Brian Jones a ride home, and we sat out in the car talking for a while afterward."

"Oh." She didn't know what to say. She couldn't imagine a parallel, any way to link that to her own experience. Sometimes people stopped coming to the dream group. It was just too much. But often they returned in a few months and simply picked up where they had left off. That was okay.

She ran her fingers over his forehead, then his eyelids. She thought of all the nights she had spent with this man, how well she knew his body, his habits. He must want her. It had been a while.

She bent to kiss him, but he opened his eyes. "What did you dream?" he said, gesturing to the journal with his head, his brows.

He never asked that. "You're changing the subject."

"I didn't know there was one. What did you dream?"

"I was in this meadow," she began, and the feeling of the dream rose up around her. "Lovely, spacious, green grass and birds singing. A friendly snake!" She giggled. "I'd forgotten that. Anyway, I think we were going to have a picnic. Or something." She let Lila give him a sultry look. "I was kind of skipping around, looking for the best spot, and then I saw these cracks appearing in the ground. I went over to you and noticed for the first time all these gray dunes behind you, regular ones, like scallops against the sky. 'Hurry over this way,' I said, because the cracks there were getting deeper, but I thought if we moved farther over we might still have our picnic. But you wouldn't move."

He looked at her, brows raised a little.

"You just wouldn't. I kept saying, 'Finn, come over here where the ground's better,' but you just looked at me. Like you are now. And the crack widened until I could see into it. I got scared. And then I woke up."

He was silent.

"I guess that's why I jumped like that when you came in. And there you were, right by me in our own bedroom." She lifted one hand, so dry and familiar, and kissed his thumbnail.

"I suppose you've figured out some meaning," he said.

She put the journal into the nightstand by her bed, added the pen, and shut the door. "I'll have to give it some thought. The cracks in the ground are pretty obvious, and I certainly was ineffective in persuading you to come on that picnic with me."

She looked at him, lying on the bed still wearing his untied shoes. "Maybe the dream was prophetic." Remorsefully, she gave Lila the night off. "And to think I had a perfumed bubble bath by candlelight."

He shook his head a little and smiled. "It was your dream, Susy. Why didn't you just jump over the crack and come to me?"

They stared at each other until Susanna felt everything give way beneath her like an elevator floor. "I'll blow out the candles," she said, not wanting to waste them. Behind her, one foot felt for steady ground.

THE SPIRAL STAIR

"DON'T TELL THAT STORY TONIGHT," GINA SAID, TALK-
ing around the dull pink lipstick with bluish undertones.
She snapped the lipstick closed and slid it into its slot in her
plastic makeup box.

"What story?" Ken asked. "Hey, don't zip up yet. Let me
help you."

Gina gave him a look and pulled up the zipper on the back
of her aqua dress. "I don't have time for your kind of help," she
said, mock-sternly.

"Don't have time? If there isn't time for that, what is there
time for?"

"Checking on dinner and running the kids over to the
sitter's. Come on, Ken. It's *your* boss coming. So to speak." Steve
Simpson was counselor in the bishopric over the children's Primary where Ken supervised the Blazer scouts.

"Oh, yeah? I thought you were my boss." He grabbed her,
tipped her backwards over his arm and kissed her until she was
breathless when he stood her upright again. She wiped a hand
over his mouth, then reached for her lipstick again.

"It was your idea to invite them, wasn't it?" he said, watching her.

She drew the lipstick on carefully, then blotted. "Well, we've talked about it off and on. They did have us over to their Christmas open house."

"I think you're just buttering up the next bishop," he said. "And, frankly, my dear, I don't think you stand a chance of being made counselor."

She stuck out her tongue at him. "Why not? Shauna Simpson's only been in the ward six months longer than I have!" She used her bratty voice, the one she never let the children hear.

Predictably, he laughed. "Maybe so! But her husband's been ward clerk and counselor. Yours only teaches the Blazers. Maybe YOU don't give him enough support to hold a leadership position." When she gasped, he threw both arms over his head and yelled, "Help! Save me! Mommy's going to brain me with her hairbrush."

There was a silence from downstairs, then Richie piped, "What's got your brain, Daddy?"

"Get ready to go," Gina called down. "Time to go, Richie." She turned to Ken. "But my husband's the best home teacher in the stake. And Steve Simpson's the one who recommended that you talk at stake conference, you know."

"No kidding?" Ken preened past her into the mirror. "Ah, he just likes my wavy hair, my big green eyes." He waggled his eyebrows at her suggestively. "Okay. You've convinced me I'm better leadership material than Steve Simpson. Now all you've got to do is convince the powers-that-be, because he's running for office. Or maybe you can get a revelation on women and I'll learn how to bake those weasels in the oven down there?"

"Weasels! That does it. Get out of here, you peasant. You're slowing me down."

"Merciful piranhas," Ken mocked, "we can't have that." He was gone, running down three stairs at a time.

"Nicki, Micky and Ricky, you're about to be kidnapped!" she heard him call, over the thunder of his shoes. Richie's shout, hollow as it blew up the stairs, was joined by the twins' squeals. In a minute the swish of the front door left the house amazingly quiet.

Nicki, Micky, and Ricki. The names jangled in her head like one of Richie's riddles. Had Ken anticipated those rhymes all the time she pored over various name books until they decided on Nicole, Michael and Richard? Now they were starting to answer to Ricky and Micky and Nicki individually, not just when he ran them all together or called them the three little pigs or the three bears.

She walked downstairs, happy in her clean home full of delicious aromas. As usual, Ken had arrived just in time for the production. He helped her throw it all together, he thought. She wondered if he realized how many layers folded behind everything good in their lives. The half hour worrying about the menu, the indecisive moments at the meat counter, the regular upkeep of the house, plus company-coming cleaning. And behind that, the vitamins and doctor's visits and naps and nutritious food to produce those healthy children he'd buckle into the safest kind of car seats for the ride to the sitter.

At moments like this, when everything hovered at readiness, the layers of preparation were all worthwhile.

When her foot touched the bottom step, the doorbell rang. By the time she got there Ione already had poked her head around the back door. "All ready, sweetie?" she asked brightly.

"Just about, Ione." She stifled a sigh as Ione bustled over to the oven and peeked inside. Company coming meant this was Ione's third trip from the brick bungalow across the driveway.

"Mmmm. Those birds smell heavenly! You know, I've never tried Cornish hens in all the company dinners I've cooked! You young girls are just amazing."

Gina smiled and took a peek herself. They were nicely browned, and she turned the oven to "warm."

"Now just Steve and Shauna Simpson are coming," Ione muttered, as if she were rehearsing the dinner herself. "Mmmhmm." She nodded several times, her quick blue eyes darting over the pans on the top of the stove and taking in the end of the dining room table that showed through the door.

"Lovely, honey. Steve's over the Primary isn't he?"

"Yes," Gina said, then added quickly, "we've been friendly with them for a long time. You know how it is, you just never get around to doing these things."

Ione nodded briskly. "Sure." She pinged the lid on the pan of wild rice, but didn't open it. "It's so funny to think of Ken teaching Primary . . . always makes me do a doubletake, you know? Of course, when I was Primary president, we hardly ever had a man teach the Blazers. Once in a while for a really tough class."

"I know. Well, this is an important year for the boys, right before they get the priesthood." Gina turned on the heat under the vegetables. Maybe it was too soon? So hard to think with Ione talking to her.

"Oh, I know, dear. And I'm sure Ken is wonderful with them. But such a talented, smart young man ought to be a leader."

"Got to get a drink," Gina said, turning to the sink. Her mouth felt like paper. She drank a juice glass of cold water and smiled, trying to edge Ione toward the door. She cleared her throat. "You know, Ione, we wouldn't ever wish for a position like that. I'm sure Ken would be gone a lot."

Ione ignored that remark. "Everything's perfect. And you're twice the girl Shauna is, if you ask me. She's nice, but I never trust a woman who's that thin during her childbearing years. Something's wrong somewhere. You know she's cheating herself or her babies."

"Well, dieters like me just envy her," Gina said.

"Oh, you shouldn't. Your figure's lovely, you've slimmed down beautifully since the twins. I don't care what the fashion is, a man likes a woman with some curves."

Ione threw out her chest, and Gina smiled. Ione was old enough to be Gina's mother and probably didn't weigh more than one hundred pounds, but she did have curves.

"Well, I'll go, sweetheart. If there's nothing I can do to help . . . Fred's going to be getting hungry."

"Thanks for everything, Ione. See you tomorrow." She walked Ione to the door and returned her parting wink.

Their first week at church, the other young wives had giggled when she told them where they lived. "Oh, did someone tell you there's another member on Herald Drive?" one asked.

"Oh, I've met her already," Gina said, and they laughed again. "She's very friendly, isn't she?"

"Ve-ry," Shauna had said.

Well, Gina didn't care. Ione loved to gossip and she had too much free time, but she was Gina's prime candidate for the Celestial Kingdom. When Gina had come down with the Texas flu four months after the twins were born, Ken would regretfully kiss her goodbye and be gone to work, and Gina would stagger out of bed to get Richie ready for pre-school. Before the carpool picked him up, she'd be bracing herself against crib and dressing table to change and wash the twins. By the time the carpool horn honked, Ione was there. Gina would lie both babies in Ione's skinny arms and stumble back to bed before the first drenching sweat of the day began.

Now Gina clicked out to the dining room to inspect the table. The blue violets in the center shone beautifully against the creamy cloth and blue enamel napkin rings matched. She returned to the kitchen to toss the salad.

Ken could kid her all he wanted about her becoming bishop's counselor. She'd never hoped to hold that kind of position herself, and had no quarrel with the men and their priest-hood. All her life she had watched her mother and other women run what she considered the real priorities in religious life. Her mother had fed the hungry at the family's dining room table whether they needed food, solace, stimulating talk or just the comfort of family living. She had run a complicated homelife so well it had looked effortless, especially to Gina's father. Gina had always wanted to be like her mother, and every time she and Ken visited Utah, she made comparisons to see how much she'd grown.

Ken was the one who didn't fit the pattern, especially in this ward. He cut his own, and he was hurt if people didn't find it attractive. He was as much fun as he had been in college, but now, as then, he sometimes didn't know when to drop the joke.

She covered the salad with plastic wrap and set it inside the refrigerator. Ken should be back by now, she thought. Ken had spoken in stake conference all right. He'd wandered from the subject of home teaching and told the congregation that he was teaching the Blazers for the second time. The first time was years ago when Primary met on Wednesday. They were trying to get teachers to wear skirts or dresses to Primary, and after hearing repeated announcements, Ken had marched into prayer meeting one week in a skirt.

The congregation had loved the story. Even the high council woke up; Fred, Ione's husband, roared, slapping both knees. But Gina had felt her cheeks burn as she smiled up at Ken. It *had* been funny when it happened. But to tell the story at that moment when the whole stake looked up to him . . . oh, she saw the stake president exchange glances with his counselor. Didn't Ken know how flippant that story made him seem?

She sighed and turned the vegetables to simmer. Ken . . . he would happily teach the Blazers forever. "Just don't put me in the nursery," he'd tell the bishopric, wrinkling his nose. "I get enough crap from Nicki, Micky and Ricky."

The doorbell rang.

Steve and Shauna Simpson stood on the front porch, talking with Ken, whose arms were loaded with packages.

"Well, hello," Gina said, "what . . . ?"

"I'd have let them in, honey," Ken said, "except I have my hands full."

"Well, come in," Gina said, stepping aside for the Simpsons and fighting a sudden urge to shut the door in Ken's face. What in the world was he holding?

"Here, please sit down," she told the Simpsons. "This chair is the most comfortable, Steve."

Ken marched past her and set his load on one end of the couch. The corrugated packages tipped precariously.

"Ken . . . "

"One minute. I can explain." He was gone again, leaving the front door ajar.

Gina looked wordlessly at the Simpsons. "You mean you don't know what he's doing?" Shauna asked, and laughed nervously.

Gina smiled and shrugged. Shauna's streaky hair was perfectly coifed. Gina knew her own auburn curls looked fine, tumbling over the aqua fabric, but she wanted to run to the mirror to check. Now Ken was back with another load, panting a little. Carefully he stacked more parcels on the couch.

"One more might do it," he said. "Sorry, but I forgot to bring them in earlier. The kids all but crunched them."

"Here, let me give you a hand," Steve said.

"No, no, you sit and sniff Gina's cooking. Something elitist, I think."

"It smells wonderful," Shauna said sweetly, crossing her long, slender legs as Ken left again. "What is it?"

"Oh, Cornish hens with wild rice," Gina said, trying not to feel rattled. "Not all wild rice . . . mixed, you know. Some people don't like a lot of wild rice."

"Well, it smells delicious," Steve said, but his eyes were on the door as if on a closed stage curtain. They heard the car door slam, then Ken came in, kicking the door shut behind him.

"That's it," he said, lowering himself to the floor next to the packages. His gray slacks edged up above his socks. "Funny, it didn't seem that hard loading them up."

Gina stared at Ken. He looked back innocently. "Well," said Steve, "are you going to tell us what you've got there?"

"Oh, this? Well, I got this great deal at First National Bank."

"What deal?" Gina said ironically. She smiled at Steve and Shauna.

"Look." He reached up, grabbed a large, flat package and tore off the cardboard. "See, it's china. This is the dinner plate, I think. Pretty, no?"

They all looked at the plate, then at Ken.

"Well," he said, "I could have gotten something with roses, but I didn't think you'd like it."

"Ken," Gina said, "how much of that did you get?"

"Twelve place settings."

"Twelve place settings? Of china? We have china."

"Oh, I know, but it was free, see. If you open an account for $100, you get a free place setting. One heck of a deal. It's nice stuff, too."

"The kids' money from your parents," Gina said faintly.

"Right. Instead of putting it in their accounts, I opened twelve new ones. Next week I'll transfer it all over."

"You mean," Steve said, "you had some poor cashier open twelve accounts and give you twelve place settings of china?" He guffawed.

"Well, she gets paid for her time," Ken said a trifle huffily. "It was their deal, after all. I just went along. I hope you like it,

Gina, because we've got a lot of it. How about you, Shauna? Could you use some china? It's free."

But Shauna was looking at Gina. "Gina," she said tentatively, "something smells a little hot . . ."

Gina jumped up and ran for the kitchen. The asparagus was limp and drab, the brussel sprouts just beginning to scorch.

Everyone was so intrigued by the free china they hardly seemed to notice the overcooked state of the vegetables, and they loaded their plates. For that much Gina was grateful. As they ate, they made suggestions. "Sell the china at a flea market," Steve said around Cornish hen.

"Give it for a door prize at the next ward dinner," Shauna tried.

"You know that couple who just got married?" Gina asked hesitantly. "The Taylors, I think their name is."

"Oh, yeah." Ken's eyes lit up. "You think they could use it?"

Gina shrugged. "Well, they're still in school and just renting. Maybe they could. If they can't, maybe they can return it to a department store for something else."

Ken licked chicken glaze from his lips. "This is terrific, Gina. I'll take the china over tonight and dump it on their doorstep."

The Simpsons laughed delightedly. "Wow, what a surprise," Shauna said. "That's very nice of you."

"Oh, no," Ken said. "No surprise. I'll leave a note that says, 'Anonymously, Ken and Gina Crandall.' "

They all laughed again. "Mmmm, I'll have some more of that rice, Gina," Steve said. "This is a great meal."

Gina saw Ken grinning from the end of the table and smiled back. Okay, he was eccentric, but he was generous. Everyone was warming up. At least the china made an easy topic of conversation. Then, as soon as she relaxed, it happened.

"We're having a dinner after ward temple day," Shauna said. "Do you think it would be too expensive to have Cornish hens?"

"Oh, no," Gina said hurriedly, without thinking. "What else would you put on the menu? Something simple?"

But it was too late. Ken had caught the cue.

"Temple day. You know," he was saying to Steve confidentially, "my most jarring experience in the church happened in the temple."

"Really?" Steve asked, and Shauna turned away from Gina to hear.

"Come on, Ken," Gina said hurriedly. "That's an old story. Tell them what Jeremy said during your lesson last week."

"Tell us both stories," Steve said with a sigh, wiping off his mouth and settling back in his chair. "Gina, that was a superb dinner."

"Well, it was in the Salt Lake Temple," Ken said. "It was one of my first times. Third time, maybe, right?"

They nodded. Gina laid down her fork. Only her plate still held food.

"I'm sitting in the Creation Room by this old guy, silver hair, the whole bit. I'm sitting there trying to get real spiritual."

Ken put on his most sincere face, and the Simpsons suppressed giggles and nodded.

"So the ceremony's going on, and I'm really concentrating, and this guy leans over and says, 'Look at the blond on row two.' "

"What?" Shauna said.

"Yeah. Really. So I look over and here's this really good-looking girl, maybe about nineteen years old. I nod, a little confused, and start concentrating again.

"Then we all stand up to move to the next room, you know, and the women are passing first and this old gentleman jabs me in the ribs and says, 'Did you see the redhead?' "

He waited for the laughter; it sounded a little nervous now. "Really. I couldn't believe it. But I try to be polite. I nod and think about what just happened in the ceremony. But this goes on all the way through. Then finally, we're almost to the end of the whole thing, and he leans over once more."

Ken paused dramatically and smiled. Gina sighed and shook her head.

"What?" Shauna said. Steve grinned.

"He leans over again and says, 'Nice sitting by you,' gets up and goes to the veil. He's a temple worker."

"Oh, no!" Shauna gasped.

"On the women's side of the veil," Ken finished. There was a silence.

"Why don't we move out to the living room and we'll have dessert later," Gina said.

She carried dishes into the kitchen and took ten deep breaths, then drank a glass of cold water. She rinsed her hands in cold water and pressed her fingertips to her eyelids, then found a smile to wear back. She didn't dare stay away, but as she walked to the living room she imagined in just an hour or two sinking into a tub of hot water, checking her slumbering cherubs, then going into the bedroom and smothering Ken.

"I can't believe you're not going to help me load this china," he said. "You're the one who doesn't want it around."

"Well, I was going to get the dishes into the dishwasher and the dining room straightened before you bring the kids back. I'm tired, too."

He looked hurt and took the first load out to the car. Gina sighed, picked up a stack of corrugated packages, and followed.

"Look at those stars," Ken said, throwing her a smile over his shoulder. "Here, put it in back and we'll drop it off before we get the three little pigs."

"Okay."

When she stepped back from the car, he caught her by the shoulders. "Kind of romantic out here, no?" he mumbled into the hair by her right ear.

"No," she said. "Come on, let's get the rest."

They were both nearly silent driving to the Taylors' place. Gina sat in the car, resting her aching head against the window as Ken made three stealthy trips to the porch and stacked the china in front of the door. The lights in the back of the apartment were on.

By the time he shot a finger to the doorbell buzzer, then raced back to the idling car, knees pumping willy-nilly, she couldn't help laughing.

Ken made the tires squeal as they pulled away. "That ought to bring them."

"They'll think it's the mafia," Gina giggled.

"They'll call in the CIA to check for a bomb. I can see it now. They unwrap a dinner plate, and KAZOOM! A living room full of porcelain powder."

"How did you know china is made out of porcelain," Gina murmured.

"Common knowledge," he said, and squeezed her knee. "Still mad?"

"This is the turn," Gina reminded him. "No. But I wish sometimes you'd been raised Mormon."

"Oh, yeah? Why?"

"Because of your crummy sense of timing."

He stopped the car in front of the sitter's and turned off the lights. "You're not supposed to aspire, babe."

She looked at him in the darkness for a full minute. "Don't give me that," she said.

He looked away, and she saw his jaw square, then harden. "I try to be a good person," he said then, sounding younger than she had ever known him.

"You are!" Her throat hurt like it had when she was a child, misunderstood and unable to explain. Ken swung out of the car. In silence, she walked with him up to the front door to collect their children.

"I thought I was pretty darn good tonight," Ken said later, running a finger down her spine until it reached her nightgown. A pause, then the finger slipped underneath.

"Oh, sure," she said. "Don't ever be awful." Now she could say it.

He moved closer. "Oh, yeah? What do you mean, huh?" He buried his face in the soft fabric between her breasts. She grabbed his curly hair with both hands.

"Oh, it's just . . . " She pounded a fist on his back. "Why do you have to tell that story? I asked you not to tell it."

"Oh, you meant *that* story." He slid his hands down her body and pulled her against him.

"Well, what did you think? You're always telling that story."

"I thought you meant the one where Eldon had a gas attack during the sacrament."

"Oh, gosh. Well, yes, I'm glad you didn't . . . Ken, aren't you tired?"

"Nope."

She held him close. "You know what?"

"What?"

"You're the one who's aspiring. I can tell."

"Not to be bishop, though," he said, and turned out the lamp.

That night Gina dreamed of a long, spiral staircase, ivory-colored with gold trim. It was the kind of staircase she'd imagined walking down when she met dates for school proms, or, eventually as a bride. But their family home had been all on one floor, and she and Ken had married in the temple, her satin dress half-hidden under the temple clothing. In the temple there had been a veil to pass through, an altar to kneel beside, but no ivory staircase.

She hadn't even thought of such a staircase for years. Their narrow stairs that led from bedrooms to kitchen were the open kind she'd never really liked. As a child, she'd feared falling through steps like those, and she noticed that Richie negotiated them carefully. They were blocked from the twins, top and bottom, with folding gates.

In her dream, Ken was waiting at the bottom of the staircase, arm extended. Smiling, she took his arm, and they began to ascend the stairs. She was happy, so happy. But then the dream's pastels became muddy. Although they kept climbing, they seemed to go no higher. They ran, then ran faster, but it was like running up a down escalator and she woke frustrated and breathing hard.

Sunday morning Ken and Richie looked like carbon copies in their blazers, ties and polished shoes before Gina had Michael and Nicole dressed and pacified. She put them in separate playpens for safekeeping. "Don't give them one thing to eat!" she warned Richie, making sure Ken could hear. Nothing was more discouraging than being ready to swoop them up and head for the car, only to find melted cracker from their noses to their bellies.

She raced upstairs to take off her duster and put on her dress. Then she slipped into her heels and looked in the mirror. She was substitute chorister that morning in Relief Society, as well as sacrament meeting. Absentmindedly, she lifted both arms and sang, "Welcome, welcome, Sabbath . . . " She stopped. She raised her arms again, bringing her right hand down on the beat.

She flushed, staring. She'd never realized she looked so. .. well, sensuous! Her figure was fuller since the twins. And her hair and cheeks and lips were all so bright, just naturally. Oh merciful piranhas! she swore, borrowing Ken's favorite curse.

She ran to the closet and hunted through it frantically.

"Honey?" she heard Ken call.

"Just a minute!"

She pulled on a loose, white, cardigan vest and checked the mirror again. Better. But still, she was so vivid. The flush in her face might fade, except with all this hurrying it might not.

But her hair. Did those tumbling curls look like they belonged on the mother of the ward?

Quickly, with trembling hands, she braided her hair and coiled it at the nape of her neck, adding a narrow, gray ribbon. Then she all but ran down the stairs, heedless of her high heels.

She looked properly demure walking to the front of the Relief Society room. The organist, who'd already begun the prelude, breathed an obvious sigh of relief as she approached. Not until the lesson began did she feel that she'd really caught her breath.

Gina, seated on the stand facing the congregation, knew her thoughts weren't attuned to the sermon, but this was the third meeting and she was tired. Ken was sending her signals with his eyebrows. The twins were fussy. She lifted her hands, open, an inch from her lap, indicating he could send one to her on the stand, but he shook his head. Richie smiled at her. He would come, but he wasn't the problem. Now Ken was pointing a thumb over one shoulder. He wanted to take the twins out, maybe home. She frowned, shook her head slightly. They were all right, just fussy. But just then Nicole deliberately dropped her pacifier on the floor and wailed. Ken was on his feet, a twin looking back placidly over each tweed shoulder. Richie snatched up the pacifier and trailed them, piping distinctly, "Here it is, Daddy."

Gina sighed. She could take care of the children better than Ken. If he had just lasted until after the sacrament song, she could have come down to sit with them until the closing hymn. Maybe, she thought suspiciously, he'd just seen his chance and taken it. Now she'd might as well stay on the stand.

The meeting ended with a reminder to vote in Tuesday's election and the announcement that next week's sacrament meeting would be under the direction of the stake president. A rustle swept through the pews. Gina saw Shauna smile at Steve, several seats from Gina, then look steadfastly into her lap. After the closing prayer, she passed Shauna and her children coming forward to meet Steve.

"Next week should be interesting," Shauna said brightly.

"Really. Any rumors or ideas?"

"No, not really."

Gina thought she looked a little smug. Was she so sure, then, that Steve would be included in the new bishopric? "Will Steve be glad to be released as counselor?" she asked.

"In some ways," Shauna shrugged. "But he's enjoyed it. Say," she said, turning back and talking over her shoulder, "what if it's Ken?" Her tone made it clear that she had never entertained such an idea before, this was clearly a joke.

Gina rolled her eyes as any wife would. "It's a big commitment."

"Oh, I know! See you later, Gina."

Gina walked out of the chapel tired and angry. Why was it so funny to think that Ken might be asked to serve in a bishopric? What did they think he'd do? Tell jokes at a funeral? Bless babies upside down? Conduct sacrament meeting backwards? He wasn't a fool, after all. Just because he wasn't a straight-arrow like Steve and some of the others who prayed in voices four times deeper than they said hello!

Ken made it a habit to call Gina every noon before he went to lunch. "Gina," he said when he called Wednesday, "I thought maybe I should tell you I might be interviewed on the radio this afternoon."

"You are? About the steel audit?"

"No, no, something else. Nothing important. Just tune to WSSI if you happen to think about it around three o'clock."

"Okay. I have to drive Richie's carpool then. I'll try to remember."

"Good. How's everything else going?"

"Fine. The twins just went down for a nap. I'm going to put away the patio furniture."

"If you'll wait until the weekend I'll help you. I don't think we'll get bad weather before then. It looks like August out there now."

"I know . . . hard to believe it's November, but you might be busy this weekend. Who knows? Ken, why are you being interviewed."

"It's something about the election yesterday. Talk to you later."

"Grrr!" she said to the humming receiver in her hand. If she were going to be interviewed on the radio this afternoon she'd be making notes, preparing little speeches in her head, pacing up and down the living room in front of the picture window. But Ken? No problem.

She went outside to put the rattan chairs and tables in the garage, but got sidetracked by Richie's toys and rubble. For such a neat little boy, he certainly could mess up a yard. "RICHard," Ken would shout if he saw it. "What is the explanation for this?"

Ken was hard on Richie, even though Richie was almost too good, Gina thought. Nicole had a wicked chuckle, and Gina thought she might have Ken's wacky sense of humor when she got older. Michael would follow her into trouble without a second thought. But Richie was serious, intent. Gina was glad to see him make a mess sometimes. Ken seemed to expect in his son whatever he let lapse in himself.

She took off her jacket. It really was warm. She lay back in a chaise, dimly aware that her thoughts were mixed with sleep. She was thinking, then dreaming again of the spiral staircase, but this time Richie was playing on it. She would boost him to the bottom of the bannister, and, with a whoosh, he would ride up it backwards, landing at the very top. Groggy, she shook the dream away, as the twins' cries through their open bedroom window woke her. What time is it? she wondered, hurrying in to change and feed the twins, then strap them into car seats in the van.

She had dropped off the three other children in the carpool before she remembered to turn on the radio. "Daddy might be on the radio," she told Richie, turning the dial to WSSI. The news had begun.

"Why? Why might Daddy be on the radio?"

"I don't know, Richie. Let's listen."

"Why don't you know?"

"Daddy didn't tell me. Hand Nicole her book, please. Now, ssh. Let's listen."

Ken was not on the news, though. He came sandwiched between a popular ballad and the traffic report.

"And now," the announcer said, "we're taking you live to Ken Crandall, a local CPA who called to concede the race for lieutenant governor in the election yesterday."

"What?" Richard said.

"SSH." Gina listened so hard she almost crowded a Volkswagen out of the right lane. She let it pass, then pulled into a parking lot, leaving the motor running. "Listen," she breathed.

"Ken? Ken, are you there?"

"I'm here, Joe. How are you?"

It was Ken, all right, bright and jovial. She heard her breath go out in a long sigh.

"You called us to concede the election for lieutenant governor, is that right, Ken?"

"That's right. I watched the election returns last night, and I obviously lost, so I thought I should concede."

"Funny, Ken, but I didn't hear your name mentioned."

"Neither did I."

"I see. Well, do you know how many votes you got?"

"Yes. I checked today, and, just as I thought, I got one vote. Mine."

"One vote." The announcer was chuckling now. "Don't you have a wife, Ken?"

"Well, my campaign ran into some serious problems," Ken said.

"I see. Such as?"

"I was late announcing my candidacy."

"How late?" An obvious snigger.

"Well, I didn't decide to run until I was actually in the voting booth."

"And what made you decide then?"

"Oh, I just looked at the names of candidates and realized I was as well qualified to kiss babies and eat creamed chicken as any candidate running. So I voted for myself."

"I suppose you realize, Ken, that this station is the most popular commuter station in the area."

"Of course. Why do you think I called you?"

"Yes. So while few people knew you were running, many will know you have conceded."

"Just my public responsibility, Joe. I felt I should let everybody know that I concede graciously, and I offer my best wishes to the winner . . . uh, what's-his-name."

"Right." Now the announcer was laughing outright. "Thanks for calling, Ken Crandall. And now, this."

It took a moment for Gina to realize the twins were fussing. Richard tugged at her sleeve, then her collar. She put the van in gear and pulled into traffic. She drove fast, her face burning as she imagined other drivers recognizing her as Ken's wife and laughing.

"Mommy. Mommy! What was Daddy saying?"

"It was a joke, Richie. Daddy was telling a joke."

"Oh." He settled back. "A joker," he said. "Daddy's a big joker." He put his thumb in his mouth, something he hadn't done for months. If Ken saw him, he'd scold.

The word stayed in Gina's mind. He was a joker. Why had she married him? Why hadn't he told her she was in for this kind of humiliation? It was all right for him; but he knew she wasn't up for this, he knew it made her uncomfortable. Why did he do this to her? How did she ever get into this situation, anyway?

When she pulled into the driveway, Ione came running from her front porch.

"Did you hear Ken, dear? Fred called me from a phone booth. He said his whole carpool was in stitches."

Gina's face felt stiff. "Did you like it?"

Ione laughed. "I'm glad I didn't miss it. But then everyone listens to that station. Listen, your phone's ringing! Mine has been, too. I'll get the twins. You run."

Gina took call after call, and soon her answers and chuckles grew automatic. Yes, Ken was very witty. Yes, a little wacky. A great guy. Thanks for calling. I'll tell Ken. With the telephone under her chin, she fed the twins and unloaded the dishwasher.

Once when she hung up the phone, Richie said, "Mommy, you look sad."

"Do I?"

"Why are you sad, Mommy?"

Gina took a deep breath and searched for some simple answer. "Oh, I think I lost something today, Richie," she fibbed. "I'm not sure I can find it now."

"What, Mommy? What did you lose?" His hazel eyes, so like Ken's were enormous, but serious. She patted his little folded arms.

"I'll tell you when you're older."

"I'll find it for you then, Mom. Wait and see."

"Yes," she said, "I bet you will."

The telephone rang again. It was Shauna. "I just died when I realized it was Ken," she said, laughing. "Isn't he a character?"

Gina's chin went up. "Yeah, he's great." She took a long breath. "Listen, Shauna, we're having a party . . . I mean a wake to celebrate his defeat. You and Steve just have to come."

"Tonight?"

"Sure. He can walk right into it when he comes home from work. Can you call some people?"

"Oh, sure. What can I bring?"

"It's potluck. Tell everyone to bring what's handy. I've got lots of lemonade and limeade in the freezer." Quickly, Gina gave Shauna the names of those who had called her about Ken's concession. Already she was pulling cans from the freezer and checking the supplies in the cupboard.

"Do you have paper plates and cups?" Shauna asked.

"Yes, I have plenty. Thanks for making the calls."

"That's okay. See you later. Sounds fun."

Gina was mixing barbecue sauce when she felt Ione's quick pats on her shoulder. If it had been anyone else, she would have slapped the hand away.

"You've got to help me, Ione! We're having a wake for Ken in the back yard. Can we borrow your lawn chairs?"

"Oh, yes, sweetheart, and what else? How about silverware?"

"I have plenty of plastic. Watch this a minute, okay? I'll check on the twins."

When Ken came home, the back yard was full of ward members and a few other friends, their plates and mouths full. He stopped at the corner of the house and stared, looking truly dumfounded. Gina laughed.

"For he's a jolly good fellow," she sang in her best chorister voice, and the others joined in. Within moments, Ken was flashing the victory sign above his head, shaking hands and kissing babies. Everyone was laughing, laughing with them.

When he came to Gina, he stopped. "You!" he said. "How could you disgrace me like this?"

He made a grab for her, but Gina wheeled away, and took off around the parameter of their guests. She heard people cheering, and ran faster when she realized Ken was chasing her.

She dodged a picnic table, circled the apple tree, then doubled back, Ken close behind her. "Hooray for Mommy!" she heard Richie squeal above the laughter and wisecracks.

"Traitor," Ken yelled, scooping his son up under one arm and continuing the chase.

Laughing, breathing harder, Gina threw herself flat on the grass. Head in her hands, she saw their chase on the backs of her eyelids, how their feet flickered like fish through the puddles of an improbable November sun.

SECOND TUESDAY:
LUNCH

Robyn, ARE YOU WITH US?" MARGOT ASKED SHARPLY.

Robyn looked up. The waiter was smiling slightly. His eyes condescended.

Robyn glanced around, confused.

"I'm having the shrimp salad," Wendy repeated. "So is Margot. Ginny is starving and having the luncheon steak. We're drinking water."

"Oh, the shrimp salad is fine for me," Robyn said quickly. "And toast," she added, noticing that Ginny looked a little embarrassed.

"Where were you anyway?" Wendy asked when the waiter left. "You seem a little blue."

"Oh, I'm fine." Robyn took a sip of ice water.

"Well, I am starving," Ginny said a little defensively. "And I'm playing tennis all afternoon. I'll work it off."

"No one's blaming you," Wendy shrugged. "You look super. Why should you worry about calories?"

"I was going to have a big lunch, too" Robyn apologized, "but I'm just not very hungry."

Robyn wished that this once she had invited her sisters over to her house for their monthly luncheon. True, they did enjoy going out. She and Margot could get away from their children for a couple of hours. And they all enjoyed dressing up and appearing in public together, she admitted. Heads still turned when they came in. None of them thought about that much, but it was reassuring. They did tease Wendy about being vain. Her hair was a pale, shimmering blond.

Today the restaurant seemed noisier or more crowded than usual. Robyn sighed and sipped her ice water.

"Robyn, what is the matter? Did you have a fight with Steve?"

"No, everything's fine."

"Come on. Give."

"I just had a dream last night that was very strange. One of those that hover over you the next day like a cloud."

They all looked at her expectantly.

"Well, I dreamed about Mother."

There was silence for a minute.

"Oh, here's the waiter," said Wendy. They were quiet while he arranged their plates.

"It was so strange," Robyn continued, poking a shrimp. "The dream was complicated and I can't remember much of it. But the part about Mother was so clear. You know how people fade . . . I mean even people you love, you just can't keep them clear. But Mother was so clear."

"I remember her clearly," Margot said. "I just don't talk about it."

"None of us talk about it." Robyn's voice rose slightly. "We haven't talked about Mother since her funeral five years ago." Her fork clinked against the plate and set it down. "Starting with that day we've been absolute stoics. 'Look at them,' everyone said, 'those Whiting girls. All four of them, brave and lovely.'"

"What I remember is, 'Your mother would be so proud,'"

Ginny interrupted. "I thought I'd throw up if I heard that one more time."

"Why should we talk about it?" Wendy asked. "We all shared it. We all shared all of it with Mother and then it ended. There's no sense dwelling on it."

"It's like we each have it locked away in our hearts," Margot said. "Like a treasure. We've closed that door and locked it because it hurts to . . . " Her voice caught and she grabbed her glass of water.

"Well, I'm sorry," Robyn said. "It was just such a vivid dream." She shrugged stiffly and picked up her fork.

"I wish you'd tell about it." They all looked at Ginny who had only been fourteen. She was the youngest.

"Well, there was just a little bit that Mother was in. We were having a family party. I don't know where we were, but we were outside on a slope. The kids were running all over, and we were talking, and the guys were lying around on the grass. Margot and I were trying to figure out the food and get organized. You know, the usual mad scene.

"But, somehow we had made Mother come back. We were all very happy about that. We'd grab each other as we passed and say, 'Isn't it wonderful?' Even though she was just sitting silently at a table inside a glassed-in porch where the tables were. That was the strange part. We could see her through the glass, but she just sat facing the wall, not looking at anyone. But we were so happy to just see her again that it didn't matter."

"Did she look just the same?" Ginny asked.

"Yes, except fainter. Dimmer somehow. She was so still and silent just sitting there. So sad. That was different. You never saw Mother sit down at a party."

"That's for sure," Wendy agreed.

"You know, that's what I thought the night Mother was killed," Margot said suddenly. "I thought that if she just weren't so wonderful and well-known, if she'd just been home stirring up cocoa instead of giving an exhibit, she might not have been in the accident. We'd still have her."

"That's crazy, though," answered Wendy, who also was artistic. "She could just as easily have been killed going to the grocery store. There are acid heads running red lights everywhere."

"I know that," Margot said. "That's just what I thought at the time."

"Was Daddy in the dream?" Ginny asked.

"He was there. I mean, I knew he was there, but I don't remember specifically dreaming him. I just remember trying to get things organized. And being so happy that Mother was there."

"Is that all that happened?" Margot asked.

"Well, no." Robyn took a sip of water. "I had gone outside for a few minutes, and Wendy and I were talking about how great it was to see Mother again. Then suddenly it just didn't seem fair. Mother had never met our husbands, or seen our children, or watched Ginny grow up. I wanted her really there, not just acting like a sleepwalker!"

Almost in unison, Robyn's sisters lifted their tumblers to their lips. She glanced at them and took a sip herself.

"So I went over to the glass and I banged on it. I started screaming, 'Mother, wake up! Mother! Wake up!' Then I thought, 'This is silly.' "

"I walked around the porch to the door and went in. I took Mother by the shoulders and shook her gently, saying, 'Mother, you're here. Mother, it's Robyn.' Things like that."

Ginny's glass hit the table sharply. Robyn swallowed.

"And Mother looked at me for the first time. Then she smiled sweetly at her hands, as if she wanted to be agreeable. She didn't say anything. I don't remember that she said anything."

Margot and Wendy set their glasses on the table sound-lessly. They leaned slightly toward Robyn.

"Then I pulled her to her feet. I was so excited. We went out to the lawn and I saw Margot first. I pulled Mother over to you, Margot.

"I said, 'Mother, here's Margot! Here's Margot, Mother. And this is Mitchell, her little boy.' And Mother smiled. Margot hugged her and kissed her."

They all glanced at Margot. She was watching Robyn.

"And then Mother looked down at Mitchie and her face changed. She looked confused. Hurt almost, and bewildered. She glanced around like a lost child in a group of strangers. Suddenly she seemed like a child instead of Mother."

"Ssshhh!" Wendy said. People at the near tables were watching from the corners of their eyes.

"Go on!" Ginny almost cried.

"Margot, you said, 'You know, Robyn, this really isn't Mother at all.' Then I woke up."

Robyn drained her glass. The others picked up their forks. Then Margot set down her fork and folded her napkin, looked at her salad and unfolded the napkin again.

"That's awful," Wendy said. "I'd love to dream about her, though. It really looked like her?"

"Yes, it was so clear. I was so happy. Except she was so silent. Mother was never silent like that."

"It was just a dream," Margot put in. "Come on, you're not eating."

"It seems so strange that she was like that," said Ginny. "Why didn't you dream her happy? Talking away. Spinning the kids in circles like she used to spin me?"

"Spin us," Wendy corrected.

"I don't know. I was so happy that I thought she was, too. But now I can't forget the dream, and that's the clearest part of it. She didn't want to be there. We wanted her there, but she didn't want to be there."

"But that's just crazy," Wendy exclaimed. "Mother always wanted to be there. In the middle of the night — whenever. The thing I remember best is the five of us sitting on Mother's double bed giggling. I never can remember what we laughed at, but we must have spent half our time talking on that bed and laughing."

They were silent for a few minutes. Wendy took the crystal pitcher and poured more water all around. Her hair hid her face.

"I don't think I've ever dreamed about her," Margot said. "Not clearly like that or I'd remember."

"Why don't we ever talk about Mother," Ginny asked. "All of you remember more than I do. You had more time."

"It would hurt Daddy's feelings," Margot said. "Look what's happened to our lunch. Doesn't this show that we can't bring her back?"

"Margot's right," Wendy agreed. "We just can't."

"But what bothers me," Robyn said determinedly, "is that we just postponed her. We shut that door even before the funeral, so we wouldn't fall apart in front of people. Look at all that's happened to us. We left her behind."

"We had to!" Wendy insisted. "She died. Look how we've changed. Think how much has happened in five years. It doesn't do any good to think about the past."

"And you said it was Mother who didn't want to be with us," recalled Ginny, her voice trembling. "This steak is too rare," she added, pushing it away.

"Our children don't know her," Robyn said, then had to stop talking.

"Robyn," Margot said very softly, "finish so we can go."

"Dreams are so strange," Wendy observed. "I guess it's good we don't believe in them."

"Here comes Daddy." Ginny brightened. "We're playing tennis at the club."

"Don't mention this to Daddy," Margot said. "Robyn feels better now."

"Sorry if I spoiled lunch. I guess I should have called and said I couldn't come."

"Don't be silly." Wendy squeezed her arm as they both stood, then put the tip on the table. It was her turn.

As Robyn left the restaurant, she had an odd sensation of being double. Some ghost of her lingered at the table with the half-filled plates and the empty pitcher, watching four young women walk away. One by one, they kissed a tall, silver-haired man who stood just inside the door, then they left.

In the sunlight, she distinctly heard the waiter scoop up the tip.

MORNINGS

FRIDAY MORNING. JUNE SKY LIKE DENIM THROUGH THE bus windows. The last day before the weekend, Marc repeated to himself, as if the words were a charm.

He swung off the bus four blocks before his stop and walked. He watched the sky behind the city's buildings, how the yellow streaks along the clouds' curves faded to cream. He watched the leaves flash in the morning breeze that was gusty enough to lift his hair and cool his throat. He made a mental note to brush his hair in the elevator.

He walked quickly, but snapped a memory of the flower banks, scarlet, periwinkle, and gold. Had they always been so vivid in June? Had he always watched the morning sky? He'd read an article the week before on terminal patients who told how beautiful the world had become, how they gloried in it as they grieved. Marc had read with a shock of recognition. Now the article haunted him. Why? he wondered. I'm not dying.

The Church Administration Building was near now and no longer towered in his vision unless he tipped his head all the way back. Marc remembered his pride when the building went up, the squared-off base, the aggressive concrete, then the arro-

119

gant height. It overshadowed the temple, tabernacle, Lion House, and Beehive House. His children could spot it from any place in the valley. "There it is!" they would shriek from the back seat of the car. "Daddy's building!"

He pushed the revolving door, as instructed by the sign. June disappeared in a rush of cool air and gleaming floors surrounding the hush of carpet. As Marc waited for the elevator, he reached into his jacket pocket for his brush.

Sister Anderson was on the elevator when it stopped. She wore a light blue dress and low heels. The dress flattered her bluish-silver hair and her sweet, blue eyes. She and the other building hostesses took people on tours.

"Why, Marc."

"Good morning. How are you?"

"Why, I'm just fine." She beamed as she watched him brush his hair. "Oh, your grandmother was so proud of those curls," she teased. "We girls thought she'd never let your folks cut your hair."

"Hair like this is really a nuisance."

"Oh, but you were such a beautiful child." She tapped his arm playfully. "That's why they always chose you for an angel in the Christmas program."

"I remember," Marc said, rolling his eyes. She laughed.

"Poor boy," she said gaily as the doors hissed.

Marc stepped out of the elevator. His office was in the missionary department. He was two minutes early. Exactly right.

It was ten o'clock before the telephone rang, but by the way his heart caught, Marc knew he had been waiting. It was Nancy, a college friend who'd worked with him on Eugene McCarthy's presidential campaign. Lately he and Kris seemed to run into Nancy and her husband everywhere, at every party, fireside, discussion group. The four became friends.

"Marc," Nancy said with her usual energy, "I'm working

with a committee here at BYU to give input on women in the missionary program."

A ragged, familiar click muffled her next words. Marc listened through a light etching of static. " . . . you remember we talked about it a little at Judy's house?"

"Oh, yes."

"Well, it's crazy, but I can't seem to get current statistics. I've talked to the staff in the managing director's office, but they just put me off. All I need to know are the percentages, Marc. The number of women who go, their ages, the number of baptisms and so on."

It sounded so simple. Careful, Marc thought, and took a breath. It was always safe to repeat. "You've discussed it with the managing director's office?"

"Have I discussed it with them! Listen, Marc, could I get those figures from my stake president, or a mission president, or a regional representative or anyone like that? They're not confidential, are they?"

Careful. "I don't know what their official status is. Let me ask around and see what the problem is."

But she would not be put off. Couldn't she hear the static on the line or, if not that, the distance in his voice?

"Oh, we've tried all that. Martha tried, too. She got Dr. Ehlert to call. It's no use. I just wondered if you have that information available, and if it wouldn't cause you any problems to get it for me. . . . "

"Well, that's not exactly my area," Marc said.

"I know, but—"

"I'm sure the information is on computer file, but it would take someone with the right code to get it."

"Oh."

"If I become aware of any materials that have been mailed to the local leaders, I'll get you a copy. There wouldn't be any problem with that."

"Okay." She sighed. "Thanks. Say hello to Kris."

"Right. Bye, Nancy."

Marc heard her hang up, aggravated no doubt, but he kept the receiver against his ear. My turn to listen, he thought grimly. There it was—a definite click ten seconds after Nancy's. Sweat broke out across his back and under his arms.

Marc stared into the perforations on the earpiece. What I wouldn't give to get a look at that ear, he thought. He imagined himself screening all the employees in the building for a particular cartilage pattern, or an orangish tinge above the lobe, and managed a wry smile. Then he slammed his fist down on the desk.

Whose ear was it? A man's? A woman's? Someone in management? How long had it been listening? Had his jokes about Church Security brought the ear to his line as he became paranoid? No, he comforted himself, it probably was Ralph who worked three partitions away and had an eye on his job. Maybe even Betsi, the young secretary who flirted and pouted at the reception desk. When his line lit up, did she lift the receiver to listen? And if it was only Betsi or Ralph, then why this clutch in his guts?

He wheeled his chair to the typing desk and worked on reports until lunch.

"There he is," Phil announced into his curled fist as Marc approached the crowded round table in the cafeteria. "It's him, my friends, Brother Blueblood."

Marc ignored him and began unloading his tray before the last empty chair. "Hi Pete, Ben, Mike, everyone."

"Ev-eryone," Phil muttered, moving his fist to one side like a microphone that shouldn't pick up his aside. "Nonentities like me are listed as "everyone". He paused for effect. "Just because I'm not related to six different buildings at BYU!"

Phil's on a roll, Marc thought, sitting down. "Just three,"

he corrected, suddenly hungry as he poured French dressing on his salad.

"Oh, just three!" Phil tried again. "Cement and stones compose Marc's bones . . . "

"Holy heck," Mike interrupted, "who put a nickel in Phil today? Dig in, Marc. You look like today had better be Friday."

"Half over," Marc grinned, a flash of his morning walk zipping through his mind. Pete, across the table, grinned back.

"Actually, Marc," Pete said softly, "I've never figured out why you don't run for office with a name like yours."

"Think I'd get elected?" Marc asked.

Most of them, Marc knew, thought him a flaming liberal, even among them, let alone the whole of Utah. Sure enough, they all hooted and Phil slapped him on the shoulder.

"You just gotta be careful of one thing," Phil said thickly, pausing to swallow a mouthful of strawberry pie. "If someone asks you about the ERA, tell them that when the church magazines got correlated it was replaced by the *Ensign*."

Not much laughter. An old joke.

"Speaking of the ERA," said Mike, "here comes the girl who started in Genealogy on Monday. Healthy looking, isn't she?"

"What does she have to do with the ERA?" Phil asked, as the girl approached. "She's too pretty to be a libber."

"Not a darn thing," Pete said reverently, his eyes following her past their table. They all smiled.

Marc thought the girl might be eighteen, no more. Her cheeks reddened as she felt their eyes on her. Her auburn hair was swept into a barrette above each ear, and her white, cotton dress swung as she walked.

"Okay, Phil," Marc said, "when do you bring out your book on Joseph's wives? All of them. Complete with dates of marriage."

"It's in the works," Phil said, but his grin faded.

"Seriously," Marc probed. "You should share your findings with the world, not just this little table of closet liberals."

"Who's a closet liberal?" Phil snorted. "I'm just a closet moderate!"

"Actually, it's a good point," Ben said, as they warmed toward another discussion that would send them back to their departments late, their adrenaline pumping. "Who does the history belong to? To us? To the membership? To the church?" He glanced over his shoulder nervously. "I ask that philosophically, of course."

"People have trouble just living the basics," Phil said, a single line appearing between his brows. "We have access to a lot of esoteric material. It doesn't have anything to do with salvation."

"Come on, no serious stuff on a Friday," Mike objected. "We had staff meeting this morning, and I'm still overwrought."

Marc pushed a doughnut a few inches toward Phil. "You deserve it."

"Is that remark directed at my figure?"

"Nope. You're in a bishopric. You need all the quick energy you can get."

They all smiled.

"You're right about one thing, Phil," Marc said. "I'm pooped. Kris and I talked half the night. We keep doing that."

"You mean like when we were in Scouts and slept under the stars?" Mike asked.

Pete was watching Marc closely. "What do you mean, talked? Has something happened? Nothing serious, I hope."

"No, nothing's wrong. We just got into a big discussion."

"About what?"

"Oh, everything. Our kids. Our parents. Our lives before we met. Why we married—really, I mean."

"Holy cow," Phil said.

"It's amazing," Marc said. He wanted to stop explaining,

but couldn't. "One of us will say something, and there's this si-lence as a whole stretch of our lives slides into place."

"Wait. Nobody leave," Phil said as Marc collected his empty dishes. "I almost forgot. New spot quiz."

Pete groaned.

"Everyone describe yourself with one word. Hyphens al-lowed. Go."

"Over-qualified," Mike said.

"Underpaid," said Ben.

"Perspicacious," said Pete.

"Overbearing," Phil added with a sigh.

"Halfbreed," Marc said and picked up his tray.

There was a pause.

"Nope," Phil said, "you're a liberal, so that couldn't have been racist."

"You're right," Marc said. "Here, stack your trays on mine and I'll dump them."

Before Marc left work that day, he slipped three sheets into his binder, then placed it in his attache and turned the key. The heading on each page read "Female Missionaries" and the year the data represented. He and Kris were having dinner with friends in Provo. He would post a legal-sized envelope with no return address to Nancy at BYU.

Callie centered a huge plant on the coffee table as Marc set it down. He grinned at her and straightened. "Home sweet home?"

"I guess," she sighed, tucking a wisp of brown hair behind her ear. It was 10:45 Saturday morning.

"One more trip should do it," Marc said. "Do you want to ride back with us or unpack?"

"I'd better go."

"Very wise. You're better off not trusting klutzes like Carl and me." He tried to be more a friend than a home teacher, but there was always a shadow of constraint. He berated that shadow in himself.

Still, she laughed. "Thank goodness my ex took the boys today. He hasn't seen them for months."

"Kids aren't much help when you're moving," Marc side-stepped. "Come on, Carl," he called as the screen door banged behind them. "One more time."

Carl was inspecting the duplex foundation. "I can see why you'll pay less rent," he said as they all crossed the yellow lawn to the truck.

"How come?"

"The limestone is starting to crumble. Did you check the basement?"

"There isn't one, really. Just a shelf."

"Ought to look that over," Carl said, turning the key in the pickup. Callie looked worried.

"That's the landlord's headache," Marc said. Callie had enough to worry about, uprooting two little kids just to move a few blocks. At least this house was still in the ward; he and Carl could continue as her home teachers. Home teaching could be tedious, but it wasn't hard to be concerned about Callie.

The mattresses were awkward to lift. Carl insisted on hoisting the double mattress on to his shoulders, leaving Marc to steady, more than lift, the other end. After moving the washing machine, they sat on boxes in Callie's small living room, eating tuna sandwiches and drinking lemonade from styrofoam cups.

As usual, Carl seemed only half tuned to their conversation. He cleared his throat formally. "Well, Callie, now that you're just around the corner from the ward, we'd sure like to see you at church sometimes."

A little of Marc's lemonade slopped on the floor. "Whoops," he said, dabbing with his napkin. He threw Carl a dark glance. The first time they'd visited Callie they invited her to come to church. She didn't speak for several tense minutes. "My husband and I were very active before the divorce," she said finally, and that was all.

Marc had been afraid she'd never let them in again, so he talked Carl into avoiding the subject of church attendance. Marc and Callie discussed books, politics, Callie's children, and her struggle to support them. Carl usually said little.

"I guess you remember what time the meetings are?" he asked now.

Callie's cheeks flamed. Marc stood. Why doesn't he just hand her a bill? he wondered.

"I think so."

"Callie, I forgot to bring back the Chaim Potok book you loaned me," Marc said hurriedly. "But will you trust me for the other one anyway? I'll bring both the next time we drop by."

Callie looked at him blankly before her eyes responded to the shift in topic. He saw her brows, her mouth, relax. "Sure," she said. She almost smiled as she looked around the living room. "But which box?"

"Oh . . . " He glanced at the stacks of boxes and felt blood in his face. "Of course. Okay," he began again, edging Carl toward the door, "you unpack and I'll find your book."

"It's a deal."

Marc reached past Carl for the doorknob.

"Thanks again," Callie said.

"Any time," Marc waved, and then they were on the porch.

Marc was halfway into the truck before he noticed he still had Callie's house keys in his pocket. "Go ahead," he told Carl. "I'll jog home. Do me good."

He saw Carl shake his head as he drove away.

Callie said nothing when she took the keys, just stared at them in her hand.

"Well, see you," Marc said, moving away.

"Marc."

He turned back. She was twisting the keys slowly. "Marc, I can't come to church. Not right now."

He looked back at her through the screen. "Callie, it's okay . . ."

She interrupted him. Her blue eyes seemed almost black, but it might be the dimness of the room compared with the sun baking his shoulders through his shirt. "I can't talk about it yet, but . . ."

"You don't have to," he said, hoping she would.

"He beat me," she said, her voice perfectly expressionless. "He—" She stopped, her eyes staring over his shoulder.

Marc looked at her, a small, brown-haired woman, tired, hot, in jeans and an oversized sweat shirt. He was wordless. Where was Carl to ask if she wanted a blessing? Where was Kris to throw open the screen door and put her arms around her?

"Callie," he said, "I'm sorry."

She looked at him, almost startled. The glaze was gone from her eyes. She shrugged a little, tried to smile. "Oh, well. It's just that I can't. It's complicated."

"Callie, it's okay." He hoped his look through the screen, his hand against it made his words count.

"I know," she said. She touched her fingertips to the wire grid that printed his palm, then stepped back. "Thanks, Marc."

He lifted his hand, wheeled, and ran toward home.

By the time he panted through the front door, he felt better. It was quiet. No one was in sight. He looked into the kitchen and found Kris sitting by the large window that overlooked the backyard. The kitchen table was heaped with books, magazines, notes, and her Relief Society manual, as well as the children's brightly scribbled art.

"Hiya," Marc said, heading for the sink and a glass of water. "Been able to get anything done?"

"Surprisingly, yes," she said. "The boys are outside sailing their blocks in the wading pool."

Marc stepped to the window for a look. "Great. Where's Karen?"

"I think she's still in the family room. She wanted to play with the family home evening supplies, and I said she could if she just uses one packet at a time."

He dropped into a chair beside her. "You certainly look well prepared for a measly little lesson." He smiled at the way the sun lit her dark hair.

"I'm thinking of calling in sick."

"Oh, come on. You?"

She rolled her eyes toward the ceiling, then gazed at him. "Marc, it's on being involved in the community. You know how Betty and Eileen are. According to them, we should censor the elementary school library and tear down any theater that shows R-rated movies."

He laughed. "Yeah, I know. But what about that corner near the school that still needs a stop sign? And who volunteers at the senior citizens center? Who's worrying about the unfenced canals? Who's babysitting for an inactive single mother, for Pete's sake?"

"Good ideas," she said, touching his forehead with the end of her pencil as if she held a magic wand. "Did you get Callie moved? Gee, we ought to take her a casserole or something later this afternoon."

Marc hesitated. "Let's not overwhelm her." Seeing into the dark corners of people's lives wasn't easy. "Find someone else of the same description if you feel you must feed the world."

Downstairs Marc watched Karen from the doorway and wished he had film in the camera. Three dolls and a hairy chimp were propped against an overstuffed chair facing Karen and a flannel board covered with cutouts of Joseph Smith.

He listened to her artificial voice as she pretended to teach, and winced. Did he and Kris sound like that? He was about to warn her he was there when one bare foot kicked the base of the flannel board. It flopped forward, the figures fluttering around it.

"Karen?"

She turned and glared at him. He crossed the room and sat down beside her on the floor. "Something wrong?"

She didn't answer.

"You were telling stories about Joseph Smith?"

After a minute she nodded. Her lower lip came out. His mind raced. What could it be?

"I found out what they did," she said, her voice accusing.

"What who did, Karen?"

She looked up, her eyes angry. "They shot him, Daddy. They killed him."

"Oh." Marc leaned back against the chair, pulling her with him. "I know they did, baby."

"Who did it?"

"Well, a mob of men came at the jail he was in, and there was a gunfight. They shot Joseph."

"But who? What were their names?"

"I don't—I don't know their names, Karen. The men painted their faces so no one would know them."

He didn't dare touch her, her control was so fragile, but he scooted a little closer. "Karen, they didn't understand Joseph. They thought he was wrong. They thought he was bad."

"They didn't have to kill him," she said, and suddenly she was crying.

He gathered her in. "Well, Joseph went to heaven," Marc began.

"I don't care!" she shouted, then sobbed harder.

He pulled her on to his thigh and held her so her face wet the front of his shirt. His hands cupped her small ribs, his fingers soothing the shaking.

"They didn't have to kill him," she said again, the words jerking and falling.

He held her hard, suddenly unable to separate her pain from his own, familiar now like a wound at the very core.

"I know," he whispered. A cutout of Joseph in the sacred grove lay near his knee, another of Joseph in military regalia just beyond it. He closed his eyes, pressed his face against her curls. "I know," he said again, "I know, I know."

Marc woke in a cold sweat, the dream alive in his mind. He checked the clock. Sunday was the only morning the alarm did not ring at 6:00, but it was only 6:30. He stared at the ceiling, then swung his feet to the floor. More sleep wasn't possible, tired as he was.

He dressed looking at Kris's dark curtain of hair. He hoped her dreams were good. The carpeted stairs were quiet under his loafers, and he let himself out the back door.

Immediately he was glad he was up. The sky was peach and robin's egg blue. The birds exercised their morning voices. Flowers and grass were dewy, but the air was already warm. The day was going to be a scorcher.

He unwound the hose and attached the hand sprinkler, watering the vegetables, then the flowers. He arched the spray so millions of glittering needles became fireworks, disappearing mid-air in the shade.

Marc could smile at what he could remember of the dream, rather like a spy novel. In it, he was working intensely, and the sense of danger was high. Now he couldn't recall what he and the others were trying to gain or protect. Clearest in his mind was the segment that woke him. He'd been whispering confidential information to a key friend in the network, standing almost toe to toe.

With a jolt that sent spray on to the leaves of the peach

tree, Marc recognized the man—Bishop Thomas! The bishop who had sent him on his mission. Now Marc concentrated. He'd been telling the bishop the heart of the plot, he remembered. And the bishop was listening, looking past Marc to something else. There was a shift in the dream then, some small interruption, and Marc paused. In that space, he caught the bishop off-guard. A change, a shadow, passed over the familiar, homely features, and suddenly they were sinister.

In that instant Marc knew with a sickened heart that everything had changed. He felt himself spin into reverse gear as the bishop's eyes turned back to meet his own. Marc looked deep. Yes, behind that friendly regard there was a knowing—a sneer?— he had never seen before.

Close to panic, Marc groped for a counterplot fast and convincing enough to fend off this double agent. Everything was in jeopardy, he realized, as his tongue swelled in his mouth. He woke, icy.

Marc sprayed the water high into the air and watched it fall. He could read the dream easily enough. He needed a week's vacation to relax, play with the kids, play tennis with Kris, fix up the yard, and get everything into perspective. But that would subtract a week from their California vacation to visit Kris's folks. He couldn't do it.

He caught a movement from the corner of his eye and looked up at the back wall of their split-level house. It was one of the children, lifting the wicker blind with one arm. The Sunday rush was beginning. He turned off the tap, wound the hose quickly, and slipped back into the house.

At first he thought Kris was still asleep. He lay down carefully beside her without touching her. She turned, raised her head, and looked at him. "Morning."

He slipped an arm under her shoulders and kissed her forehead. "Sleepy?"

"No." She sat up suddenly and faced him, her legs curled under her. "I've been thinking."

"Oh," he said. Hardly an adequate response, but he would rather close his eyes right now and touch than hear and think. There has been too much, he told himself, too much to think about.

"Marc?"

He opened his eyes and managed a smile. "Thinking seems pretty strenuous this early in the morning."

She regarded him steadily. She had been thinking.

"Are you all right, Marc?"

"Sure. We're always thinking these days, aren't we?"

"I guess so. I feel like I'm on a hanging bridge. I hate it, but I can't go back, and for some reason I don't want to reach the other side. Do you know what I mean?"

"Yes." He laughed. "You just reminded me of the fast one Phil pulled at lunch Friday." He told her about the one-word descriptions.

"And you said 'halfbreed'?"

"Yes, I did. Brother Blueblood."

She said nothing. Her green eyes filled. He took her hand, and her tears and words came at the same moment.

"But Marc, you are honestly the best Mormon I know." She shook the tears off, swallowed, and lifted her chin challengingly. "I'm the halfbreed. A convert. I can remember what it was like to be outside the church in all that space."

He raised his eyebrows, opened his arms again. She snuggled close, but didn't miss a beat in the conversation. "I've been thinking about it. It's hard to explain, but in college—when we met—"

"I remember," he said, sliding his hands under her nightgown.

"I knew I wanted to dance. I knew I wanted my degree. I

assumed I'd marry some day, but there were so many other decisions, so many paths to follow. Do you see what I mean?"

"I'm not sure." He stilled his hands. His mind felt still, too, weighted and weary.

"Well, with you—you were always so sure. You knew you'd go on a mission and you went. Later you knew you'd get married and have a family. You knew you'd finish school, and then a good job would come along. I mean you knew all that."

"But it was what I wanted."

"I know. But you never really considered anything else. Do you see what I mean? Those had always been the things you would do." She sighed and gave up. "Oh, I can't explain it."

"But wait." He propped himself on an elbow so he could see her face. "Have you always felt like a halfbreed? When you joined the church, you did the expected things, too. Got married in the temple, had a baby, then another baby, then another baby." He stared at the front of her nightgown.

"I get the point!" she said, shoving his elbow suddenly so it slid from under him and brought him down beside her. "I know. That's what I mean. Then I joined the church and I wanted to be a thoroughbred like you."

"Do you still? Do you want to feel all the way Mormon?"

Her eyes left his and looked out the window opposite the bed. "What does that mean?" she asked vaguely. "Mormons say you're with them or against them. Us, I mean. One way or the other. So either I am or I'm not. What does how I feel have to do with it?"

"How we feel seems to be everything these days."

She sighed. Then she sat up and looked hard at him. One hand smoothed his forehead, her fingers passing lightly over his eyelids. "But you, Marc. You're not a halfbreed."

As Marc waited on the bench for sacrament meeting to begin, their son Nicky was on his knee and Ryan squirmed restlessly beside him. It was hard to get the boys through three hours of meetings with the hardest meeting last, so Marc wouldn't let them take out their books until the meeting was well underway.

Where was Kris? he wondered for the twentieth time. Karen had gone to look for her, but neither had returned. Marc sat Nicky on the floor and blocked the aisle with his knees. A hand punched his shoulder and he looked up. It was Pat Moran, beaming at him.

"How you doing, Marc?"

"Fine, Pat. How are you? Have you seen Kris?"

"Oh, she's coming. Hey, tell her for me she did a good job with the lesson. Tell her not to let them get her down."

"Who?"

Pat laughed as if he'd cracked a joke. "There are some of us who really appreciate her lessons. I think she could persuade me of anything," she said, without answering his question.

"I'll tell her." Pat swayed down the aisle clutching a child with each hand. A baby rode her shoulder, and a diaper bag was slung high on the opposite shoulder. Her older daughter carried Pat's purse over her small shoulder, with both hands steadying it against her thin side. Pat was expecting another baby soon. She looked like Mother Earth, Marc thought with a smile. Kris looked frail in comparison, pregnant now for what they'd agreed was the last time. They hoped for another girl.

Soon Kris would take a casserole to the Morans, conveniently packaged so it could be used immediately, refrigerated a day or so, or frozen. And a few months after that, Pat would be on their doorstep with a huge peanut butter jar full of her applesauce cookies.

"No, Nicky," Marc said, reaching to pull up his socks. He set Nicky on his knee firmly enough that the boy's light curls bounced. Nicky stared at him as if he were being unreasonable.

"You're right, Nick," Marc said. "It is unreasonable. So humor us." He kissed Nicky's head. With these curls, he thought, this kid will end up playing the angel in Christmas pageants, too.

Marc recalled the Christmas party for the elders' quorum. A bunch of them got on the subject of who should do the dishes. Later, as Marc scooped potato salad onto plates, Pat had poked him in the chest. "You know what?" she'd asked, loudly enough for the entire line to hear.

"What?"

"I guess you know I'm not pro-ERA," she grinned, "But I sure wouldn't mind having a husband who was!" She burst into laughter, and everyone in earshot laughed, too.

There was Kris, entering the chapel with Karen by the hand. He looked at Kris closely. She was smiling. It wasn't until she faced him, sliding past him into the pew, that he saw the glitter in her eyes.

"I told you," she muttered, still smiling. She sat down on the far side of Ryan, who was slowly falling asleep. She moved still farther down the bench and adjusted Ryan's position so his head was cradled on his arm.

Marc nodded toward Ryan and winked at Kris as the bishop's counselor began the meeting. One fewer to contend with, the wink meant. Kris stared a second, then smiled back, but her mouth was tense. She looked away. Marc felt butterflies squirm in his stomach, empty since it was fast day.

The welcome. The opening song. The opening prayer. Announcements. Three babies to bless, one baptized child to confirm. The sacrament song. The deacons took their places along the aisles and the noise level dropped.

The bread tasted slightly stale, Marc noticed. He held the tray for Nicky, then Karen, then Kris. He handed Nicky a new book, once the tray was gone, and tried to concentrate on the state of his soul.

The list began. This morning he'd seen to the garden and lawns, talked with Kris, helped dress the children, led a discus-

sion in the elders' quorum, paid their monthly tithing, volun-
teered for next week's welfare farm assignment, signed up for
the monthly temple day. He'd avoided controversy when the
subject of polygamy was raised in Sunday school. He waited,
but felt no glow of blessing.

Okay, Marc thought. I'll settle for the approval of my fellow Saints along these benches. We give that to each other, week
after week, the recognition we're doing what's right. We're here,
we believe, we tithe, we serve. He looked at Nicky, who was
using his fingers to burble low sounds, and amended, we en-
dure.

But he caught sight again of Kris's tense neck and shoulders. And we judge, he added. He closed his eyes for a second
and sighed. They do. I do. Each other and ourselves.

As far as Marc could tell, his fellow Saints knew the same
God he'd always known—the God one approached on one's
knees, confessing all one dared, always tarnished. Maybe that's
why we need to meet so often, Marc thought. We reassure one
another.

But his new God, the secret one he'd encountered by accident recently, cared nothing for his rationalizations, his recrim-
inations, his inadequacies. If he began that sorry litany, this God
withdrew. No, he had learned that all he could do was review
the store in his heart, and occasionally something in it would
shine. Then, bathed in a sudden radiance, he would find himself
shaping only "thank you,"—he and the God whispering "thank
you" back and forth in the intimate dark.

Marc looked up as the deacons walked down the aisles again
and realized he'd omitted something from his list. This boy,
Jason—Marc had spent a few minutes with him after he saw Jason
bolt through the lobby and out the glass doors.

"What's wrong?" Marc had asked as he approached, then
he saw Jason's scarlet face and stopped. What else could be wrong
with a thirteen-year-old boy who fled priesthood meeting?

Jason rubbed his shoes against the grass over and over, as if scraping off mud. He and his friends had bought a magazine, he said, and together they'd looked at the pictures of naked girls. Then he'd won the toss to take it home, and he'd looked at it some more in bed that night. After a while he couldn't help what he did with himself. Marc put a hand on Jason's shoulder and they talked, then went back inside.

Careful not to look directly at Jason now as he handed Marc the tray laden with cups of water, Marc rejoiced that he was no longer an adolescent. He held the tray for his family, then took a cup of water.

As Jason moved silently to the next row, it happened. Something relaxed then lit behind Marc's eyes. The bread had been dry as ashes, but the water was a thimbleful of light.

The rows of shoulders shifted. The sacrament was over. Ryan still slept on the bench. Karen reached for the book bag and removed a small box of crayons and a coloring book about Jesus. Nicky dangled from the back of the pew in front of them until Kris touched his shoulder and showed him his bottle.

Marc took Nicky and tipped him back in his left arm. What a miracle it would be if he fell asleep, Marc thought, looking into Nicky's eyes, utterly awake.

Marc stretched his right arm along the bench until his fingers touched Kris's shoulder. She smiled at him and moved a little closer. Nicky drained the last swallows of milk as noisily as soda though a straw. Suddenly he hurled the empty bottle into the air.

Marc's hand leaped from the bench and caught the bottle as it arched toward the pew behind them. He heard Kris's sigh of relief join his own as a chuckle rose from the back benches. He ducked a smile toward their friends, tucked the bottle into the book bag, and set Nicky on he bench beside Karen. He handed him a book.

The counselor conducting the meeting finished bearing his testimony to the truthfulness of the gospel of Jesus Christ, then invited the congregation to express its belief. He sat down. There was a pause.

Marc had considered sharing his feelings about the new God. But he wasn't sure that anyone else didn't already know what he'd been so slow to learn. Perhaps he'd been the only one caught at the throne of the authoritative God, whispering his bargains, his pleas. He hadn't even told Kris yet about this tentative, surprising light.

His first memory of it was after he went to lunch with his father. "I'll get the tip," Marc had offered when his father covered the tab with his hand.

Their waitress had been in her late twenties, pretty, but with dark smudges under her eyes. Her right hand wore a plain gold band, and her required high heels were scruffy in back.

Marc noticed her shoes as he reached into his wallet for the few dollars that would have bought his lunch in the cafeteria. Behind them he saw the twenty dollar bill they'd earmarked for Nicky's birthday present. He pulled it out, shielding it with his hand, and put it under the bread and butter plate.

He wrote a check for Nicky's present and worried how to justify his extravagance to Kris. They couldn't afford it.

That night in bed he found himself reviewing the day, trying to pinpoint the source of his well-being. Suddenly in the dark bedroom he saw the minor events of the day before him on a low table or altar. The guilty twenty dollar bill shone, then burst like a flare in his heart. The new God spoke to him without words.

Listening to Eileen Evans begin her remarks, Marc decided such experiences were not for relating. They were too soft, hidden, and subjective, yet clear as candle gleam.

"We had such a fine lesson in Relief Society this morning,"

Eileen was saying now, her round face smiling below her cap of curls. Marc snapped to attention. "It was about our responsibility to be involved in our community."

Marc winked at Kris, who raised her eyebrows slightly. "Of course, many of us have worked for years and years giving compassionate service. But too often we don't look past our own sisters here in the ward."

Her voice went up a note just as Marc began to relax. "I can tell you, it is a witness to me that our leaders will tell us what we can do and which issues are worthy of our concern. We know what they are!"

Marc listened to the rest disappointed. Pornography must be halted; homosexuality cannot be tolerated; abortion must be totally outlawed.

"What happened to the stop sign?" he whispered, but Kris was studying her hands, as if listening closely to an opponent in a formal debate.

He breathed more easily when Eileen sat down, and a young women he didn't know took her place at the microphone.

"Brothers and sisters," the woman began, "I am just so thankful for my home and my husband and our babies. It just makes me sick, the women who go out and work and leave their children . . . " When she steadied her voice she went on. "I'm sorry to be emotional, but I just wish every woman could be as content within her home as I am. Oh, I know it can be boring, and some days we all just about go crazy . . . " Her voice caught on a laugh or a sob, Marc wasn't sure which, and the congregation stirred with sympathy, "but we know this is what we should do."

Marc's stomach growled. Usually fasting was not difficult for him. He was used to it. But colors swam before his eyes. When his vision cleared, he realized he was angry.

He remembered an evening a few months ago when he

and Carl visited Callie. She was depressed, and Marc finally got her to tell them why.

"It's Brad. My ex. He's mad at me because I had an attorney friend call him because he didn't pay child support." She met Marc's eyes. "He threatened to move out of state and never send us another cent."

She looked at the bedroom door where her boys slept. "If he does that, we'll have to go on welfare. I can't make enough proofreading and editing to keep us alive. He's already cut the boys from his health insurance."

Marc remembered how he and Carl had shifted in their chairs. As if she understood their discomfort, Callie smiled at them.

"Oh, he wouldn't do that," Carl said.

The smile vanished. "My friend, Anne . . . Her husband did just that. She went on welfare, and the state tracked him down and made him pay. When she got a job, he quit paying and moved to another state. She couldn't make enough to have her babies tended, so pretty soon they were back on welfare again."

Then suddenly she was on her feet. She paced the length of the small room, then whirled on them. "I'll cut my wrists before I use food stamps!" she exploded.

Sitting in church, Marc remembered how he'd tried to convey friendship, but he'd felt like an enemy. What if Callie had come to church today? She'd feel herself surrounded.

Now Brother Loring was finishing up. His testimony had praised those that preceded it. He advised the sisters to heed the advice of the priesthood. Automatically mouthing "Amen," Marc felt a tug of disloyalty as if he were, again, the enemy.

Then Lane Meeks put in a few words about his newborn son, followed by several Ames children bearing rapid-fire testimony. The former bishop spoke nostalgically for a few minutes.

Marc tried to relax. His stomach churned. Adrenaline on a fasting stomach is potent, he thought. No wonder people have had psychedelic experiences during fasts.

Kris held Nicky on her lap. Marc could see she was weary. Her energy was short these days, and he guessed she'd expended enough this morning to drain her for the rest of the day.

He tapped her shoulder and held out his hands to Nicky, lifting him over Karen's lap. He fastened his watch on Nicky's round arm just below the elbow and held it to Nicky's ear. Then he closed his eyes, wishing away the beginning of a headache. He opened them again when something crossed his arm — a microphone cord.

"I heard somebody say something about a prophet," Karen's voice said loudly. "And I just want to say I know about Joseph Smith."

There was a ripple of amusement, which Karen ignored.

"I know he was a good prophet, and he never did anything bad." Marc had a sudden vision, a Karen ten years from now, her blond hair still shining, her voice strong, a determined young woman speaking her mind. He felt tears warm his eyes.

All spun around him like a film projected at too high a speed. He sat half dazed through Karen's closing "Amen" and Kris's opening, "My sisters and brothers." He felt helpless. Why must Kris speak? Why today?

He urgently wanted her to sit down, to be quiet. He held Nicky closer to keep his own hand from tugging at Kris's hem or elbow. What's wrong with me? he wondered. He was trembling.

He looked at Kris. Despite her pregnancy, just beginning to show in the tailored dress she wore, she looked almost as young as she did the afternoon he met her; the same light behind her face, the same irony that surprised her listeners into laughter. But he saw that the hand holding the microphone shook. Not like Kris.

"The church has given me a lot," she was saying. "I guess I grabbed it like a life preserver in a sea of experience! It gave me a new home, a community, a way of living. And it gave me Marc." Her voice snagged, but she smiled and swallowed.

And I gave her this morning, Marc thought in sudden horror, on which to be on the wrong side. For a second the room tilted.

True, he'd seen Kris as floundering in that sea, glad for the life preserver that towed her to his ship. Now it was her ship, too.

But for the first time he wondered if she had been swimming instead of floundering. Or floundering and swimming toward one of the many shores she'd described. While he had simply followed the easy, pleasant, right voyages that had lain charted for him all his life.

Someday — how had it escaped being today? — would she look at him and see in a blinding instant not a rescuer but a double agent who ensnared her in a hopeless plot?

He felt weak. That flash had taken only a minute, he discovered.

"I love to cook," Kris was saying tightly. "I love playing with my children. I'm very lucky to have them."

What is she doing? Marc asked himself. Then he realized she was reciting her credentials, her passport for safe passage. She didn't mention her college degree or her dancing experience.

Nicky yelled. Marc glanced down and saw that one of his hands clutched Nicky's thigh, gripping it so tightly his knuckles were whitening. Nicky yelled again. Marc shifted him to his shoulder and stood, ducking his head a little. He walked quickly from the chapel, knowing even as he did how ideally he appeared — the helpful father.

In the foyer Marc set Nicky down and stared out the glass doors. Kris's voice came from a ceiling speaker, but Marc couldn't take in the words. He was amazed to see the sky outside absolutely blue, the trees quiet. Still, there was something in the air. He picked up Nicky and went outside.

On the sidewalk in front of the chapel, Marc breathed deeply. He looked all around at the undeveloped fields that backed the subdivision and the long, two-lane streets that ran through them. He could almost see the intersection by the canal. It was at the top of a little rise. As Marc drove toward it one day last summer, he'd spotted a child bobbing and rolling in the canal.

A glance showed the intersection empty, and Marc accelerated instead of braking. He passed the child by a quarter mile, screeched to a stop, and ran to the canal's edge where he threw himself flat. He edged farther and farther out on the bank, his right arm extended. The second before the child reached him, he thought the little body would wash past, but his fingers touched cloth, he groped, got a better grip, and pulled the child — a little boy — up on the bank.

He was still working on the boy when a sheriff's car squealed beside him and the deputy sheriff and the boy's parents jumped out. Looking at the parents, Marc felt himself go limp and cold all over. He handed their boy, now crying, to them without a word.

When he detailed the story to the sheriff, he mentioned his race to the canal.

"You didn't stop?" the sheriff said.

"What?"

"There's a stop sign at that intersection. You didn't stop?"

"No," Marc said, ready to laugh at a lame joke. "I didn't stop."

"Getting in a wreck wouldn't have helped the kid," the deputy said.

"The intersection was empty. I saw that."

"Well, I won't give you a ticket." The deputy rubbed the back of his sunburned neck.

Marc, in front of the chapel on Sunday, grinned again with the same bafflement he'd felt staring at the deputy as weed scratches stung his arms and his knees trembled. What to say to someone like that? he wondered again.

Thinking that somehow brought Marc around a mental corner to what he'd tried all weekend to forget—that listening ear on his telephone at work in the church's headquarters. The static buzzed in the back of his brain.

Holding Nicky's hand, he walked to the edge of the grass and stared over the fields between the redwood fences and the swing sets. Once the fields had been alive with rabbits, he'd heard. He had a quick image of himself as a rabbit, paralyzed by the inevitable roar of authority behind two headlights on a dark road.

But half a dozen strategies erased that picture, breaking the paralysis. He pictured himself with an ear to the receiver and an eye out the door toward the secretary's desk. He imagined complaining to his supervisor about the faulty phone line. Sometimes he could return calls from Ralph's phone. Whatever the method, he need not stay still.

Swiftly Marc lifted Nicky under his arms and tossed him high into the dizzy blue sky. He felt the answering jolt on his hands spread clear into his shoulder sockets. He flipped Nicky's little body so it lay across his arms. Nicky was breathless with laughter.

Two steps to the lawn and he was swinging his son in circles high and low, around and around in the yellow day until both sprawled on the tailored grass. There they watched blue sky, green grass, and the red and white chapel circle them merrily. Any time now the church doors would open and their people, tired and talking, would come out.

BISHOP TED

MARCH 4. I JUST CAME FROM ELLEN'S HOUSE, WOR-
ried sick. It seems so ironic that both of us could lose
our men within two years of each other. As if we have the
same destiny even while living very different lives.

I remember in high school, we'd sit with a *Seventeen* magazine between us and take tests on what type we were. Both of
us thought we were "classic" and should wear tailored clothes
and sophisticated perfume. But I'd try to convince Ellen she was
the pixy type. With her little freckled face and petite body, how
could she be classic?

"But I despise that cutesy stuff," she'd say, wrinkling her
elfin nose. "But you, Cheryl, are for sure an 'earth mother.' "

And when I'd get mad, she'd shrug and say, "Well, look at
you. You're all curves, your mouth, your eyes, your ears, all drawn
with circles. You'll get married and be terrific with kids."

Then I'd hit her with a pillow and we'd tussle. Still, I knew
what she said was true, circles on circles even where she never
saw. But I still claimed to be classic.

And here we are, everything out of kilter, nothing like we
planned. Larry dead for two years after that stupid immersion

heater blew up in his face while he was "serving his country" weekends in the reserves. Making enough money to pay for Matthew is what he was doing. So one day he's with us, tinkering with the car, offering to bathe the kids if I'm ready to cut them up and flush them down the toilet, and the next morning, BLAM, a freak accident, and that's it.

And Ellen. We end up in the same ward at last, even though I'm in a subdivision full of young families and she's ten miles away in an adults-only condominium. She's finally in love for real after becoming disenchanted with dating and singles activities, completely bonkers over Anthony, whom she plans to marry. Then a car accident and *he's* dead. And she, I find out with a shock, is not only grief-stricken but in terrible trouble.

That kind of trouble used to happen in high school too, though not to us. But it still happens, I find out, and to grown women.

"So you talked to Ted," I said to her today while the kids roared around outside in the early spring sunshine. We had to talk fast since the kids wear people down, even old friends like Ellen.

"Yes. The bishop." She emphasized it because we keep forgetting to call Ted bishop. He's new, and we've both known him as just Sally's husband.

"And?"

"He says I'm not repentant."

"What's that supposed to mean?" Already I'm getting mad. And scared.

"Well, it's true." She picked up a pillow and held it against her as if anticipating what her belly will be like in a few months. "Cheryl, tell me you can understand that my memories of being with Anthony are all I have now. Those and the baby."

"Sure. So?"

"Well, I'm supposed to tell him all about that—confess it,

like something nasty. I can't do it. It may be over, but it's still the most beautiful part of my life."

"Well, but—you're not sleeping with anyone else. You're true to Anthony and he's gone. Isn't that changing? Isn't that repenting?"

"I guess not. He says a full confession and remorse. And I don't regret anything we did, especially not now that I've lost him. I'm glad we made love. I'm glad I'll have his baby. That freaks Ted out."

"The bishop," I reminded her.

I went outside to tell Karie to quit beating on Matthew. That's the thing with kids, you never know what will happen. I'd planned to have three kids all right. A tall, blond, grave son; a dark, petite, graceful girl; and then a red-haired bubbly type, either a boy or a girl. I don't know who I thought I'd marry to get such a variety, but it wasn't Larry, whose sandy hair was just three shades blonder than mine and whose gray eyes were just two shades less blue. Even then we agreed our children would have his fine round chin and my little ears. Instead all *three* of them have his sticky-out ears and my receding chin. And I never knew until Jason was born that Larry had been a rambunctious kid. Then my mother-in-law clued me in too late.

"We're leaving in five minutes," I yelled over the clamor, hoping Ellen's fellow condo-dwellers wouldn't evict her for knowing such uncouth people. On the way over I'd been tempted to drop off the kids at the little park that lies between our house and Ellen's but I didn't dare. Transients and high school kids hang out there, and I thought of syringes and perverts and just kept driving.

I closed the front door and looked Ellen in her sad, yet shining face. She's always had this glow to her as if she ate sunlight for breakfast. I decided she needed some straight talk.

"Look, Ellen. The last thing you need is trouble with the

church. I mean, it's tough being a single parent and all that, but the church helps out, believe me. You'll probably never have to use food stamps like I do, but when I run short before the end of the month, it's sure nice to get an order of groceries to tide us over."

"I know, Cheryl."

"Well, you've got to get this settled. Not just for the groceries, either. For your whole future, and the baby's."

She shook her head and suddenly tears dropped onto her twisting hands. "Ted's set a court for Friday night. I don't think I'll even go."

I sat down suddenly, as if a trap door had opened under my feet. "What? He did? You've got to go."

"I can't say more than I've already said. It would be a violation."

"Look, Ellen. This is like school—like college. Or like getting a job. Sometimes you have to tell people what they need to hear."

But her face just lit up under the tears. "I loved Anthony, and I still love him, and I'm glad I loved him in every way I could. I can't lie to myself or to the Lord."

"How about just to Ted?" I asked. But the question dropped like a soggy wash cloth to the floor, soon squished to nothing as the kids hopped through, all looking alike in their parkas and pinkish hair. I'd never imagined their dirty faces any more than I'd imagined the food stamps or Larry in the ground by the time he was thirty. We went home.

March 18. I couldn't even write in here last week. I was so upset. This journal on Sunday nights has kept me sane, but lately things have been more awful than any time since right after Larry got killed. Even more awful than when Ellen heard about Anthony.

I can't believe they did it. Ellen's out. I feel like she's been murdered, stomped into the ground. I think she does, too. It's such a slam of the door in her face. Every time I think of it I cry, and she told me before we hung up last night that the skin under her eyes is chapped.

Today I sat in church and watched the bishop all during the meeting, how he beamed so kindly down on all of us with his bedroom eyes. I've always thought he had bedroom eyes, although after he became bishop they seemed to glow more and swivel less. Ellen wasn't there. She was supposed to be, sitting through the meeting, letting the sacrament tray pass her by, humiliating herself week after week. She won't do it, and I don't blame her. But I miss her. If she's not at church, I don't see her very often.

All my kids are going to get chicken pox. I can see it coming. Half of Jason's school class is absent now. I've worked it out on the calendar, and I figure Jason will get it sometime this week, then Karie and Matthew about twelve days later. Goodbye spring.

March 25. I'm exhausted. Jason has a fever of 102, and Karie and Matthew have been wild all day. Friday I took Matthew and we ran to the store for orange juice and flour. Today I couldn't leave Jason to go to church with the other kids.

I've talked with Ellen on the phone, and she sounds grim. She said the excommunication is like mourning another death. I offered to call up the bishop and tell him he can kick me out, too, but she just laughed (sadly) and said no. I won't see her for weeks until all the pox are gone. She can't remember if she's had it.

At least her job nursing in the long-term facility is secure. Old people and crazy people don't care if she's pregnant, she says. I care. I have a feeling she'll have the petite, dark- haired girl that was supposed to be mine. Karie is built like the boys — all three as stout as ponies.

April 1. I didn't dare go to church because Jason is still scabby and the other two could break out in pox any time. If any child in the area has avoided getting exposed, I'd hate to be the one to ruin it.

A surprise happened tonight. The bishop came over. Knowing I'm Ellen's best friend, I think he was afraid I'm apostatizing to protest what he did to her. Actually, it's a temptation, but the chicken pox are keeping me housebound anyway.

Amazingly, all three kids were in bed when he came, rather late, come to think of it, and by himself. So we sat and talked. He has the most intriguing eyes. I can't remember that much of what he said, but the way he looked in between our sentences really got to me. Probably I've been shut up here too long, and I'm parched for human company. That must be it.

I still hate him, well, resent him, for what he did to Ellen, but I admit he really believes it was the right thing, the only thing he could do. And I think it hurt him.

After he left I tried to remember the last conversation I've had alone with a man, any man, since Larry died. I don't think it's happened. The pediatrician comes closest, and then the kids are always climbing on me. Of course I talked with Bishop Sorenson before Ted became bishop, but that's different. That's over a desk, not eye to eye in a room growing soft with the lateness of the hour.

April 8. An awful day. Karie and Matthew are both so sick that I promised the Lord I'll forgive their ears and chins if he'll just make them well. And I won't shout at them or spank them any more, even when they paint the refrigerator with water colors. At least I'll try.

This morning I found out I've gained another five pounds. I can't leave the house, and there's nothing here that makes me feel good except food. At least I can see through the windows that spring is really beginning outside. Eventually maybe I can take the kids and go for long walks without exposing people. Someday this will end. Maybe I'll take them to that park and push them high on the swings. Anyway, I can exercise all this blubber off. Right now it's just hopeless.

Ellen wasn't home today. I tried to call a couple of times. I thought about her and the bishop. Then I just thought about the bishop.

I wonder how much Sally loves him. She seems like the model mother-and-wife they say doesn't exist. Perfect, perfect for him. Not getting chubby like me. Still, if her kids get chicken pox, she'll probably be alone with them a lot, too, since he's busy being bishop. But not all the time. And her pleasure must entail more than peanut butter and chocolate cookies. (My newest recipe and *all* of us like it.)

April 15. At last I got out. I went to Ellen's first, with the kids' Big Wheels in the back seat. Thank goodness their grandparents sent them those for Christmas. Once the kids are all in school and I can work full-time, such luxuries won't be quite so rare. I hope.

I don't know. Ellen seemed so distant. It was only when I went to church that I figured it out. The bishop has her shine. Bishop Ted, I call him to myself, mating both characteristics in my mind—the caring, gentle man and the authority he draws straight from the Spirit. I watched him during the meeting when he wasn't looking my way, and his glow has definitely increased since he made that decision to excommunicate Ellen. And hers has gone. I think it's a confirmation for me, and despite my sadness for Ellen, I feel a hundred times better.

I watched Sally, too, and their five children. She manages them beautifully, but she and Bishop Ted seem a little distant. I know I heard an edge on her voice during Relief Society when she described all the meetings he has to attend. And she called him "the bishop." She said they've taught their kids to call him "the bishop" too, when they're at church. Even the littlest, who can barely talk.

He does have this glow, this aura of knowing what's best. I mean, before he was bishop he was just one of the husbands, like Larry and the rest. Now he's different, like the "smooth and polished shaft" you hear about in the scriptures.

April 22. I know this sounds weird, but I swear it happened. When I went into church this morning, Bishop Ted was standing by the door talking to someone. I heard my name and looked back and saw him framed by light like an aura. It was more than the sunshine outside, I know it.

Oh, I admit I've been eating and sleeping too much, like I'm hooked on both, but I'd fixed myself up, and my navy suit still fits fine. I looked nice. I just waved then, but when I got a drink and went over to the chapel, I held out my hand and met his eyes. When he took my hand, it literally burned. I don't know what my eyes said, looking back at him, but I felt heat rush down my body. I'm certain he held my hand a little longer than necessary. I'd swear it.

"How ARE you?" he asked.

He reads me like an open page. I don't really know him that well, yet I feel we've known each other in some secret way forever.

I thought about him all day, and the day went faster. The kids seemed cuter and more fun. They cuddled beside me while we read Sleeping Beauty. I fixed hot chocolate for supper. Hot chocolate gives them their milk, it's not that expensive, but they feel like it's a treat. Thank goodness the assistance check came yesterday. I always feel so desperate the week before.

April 29. During the week I've been fighting the blues by reading a couple of novels based on the early history of the church. I feel I've discovered a gold mine. Then people were so much more spiritual, so much more ready for adventure, for the unusual. Now we're all in these narrow little ruts with no way, it seems, of climbing out. Afraid of being different than everyone else in middle-class America.

For example, there are people who knew who they should marry by actual visions. One young apostle saw each of his wives' faces sometime before they'd met. So when he did meet them, he immediately knew he'd marry them.

Not that I really believe in polygamy, although you almost *have* to believe it was right back then. I do like their spiritual approach to marriage. And love.

Whenever I can I get the kids busy for a while, I read a few pages in those novels or sometimes in my old mysteries because I've forgotten who-dunnit. I even cheated the budget to buy a Harlequin at the grocery store, and I never could stand them before. I feel like an addict.

But there's just nothing else to do except housework and child care. It will be a year or more before I can get Matthew into some kind of preschool or Head Start and go to work. I probably won't earn much more than the state pays me now, but at least I'll meet people. Right now I'm just waiting it out, for something or someone to come along and rescue me. But I have my doubts about rescue. I've gained another two pounds.

May 6. I saw Ellen today. She really looks pregnant, and she's so short that it seems ridiculous. I made the mistake of trying to explain to her why the bishop had to excommunicate her, really an act of love although it seems so harsh.

She got so angry I had to gather up the kids and go. I feel badly about it, but I know I'm right. If only she'd come to church and see how loving and spiritual Bishop Ted really is. He'd welcome her back with open arms, I know.

When I listen to her side of it, I feel I'm being torn in two. I understand how she feels. But how can she bear to be so alone, not just now but indefinitely? Like floating in the Bering Sea on a tiny ice chunk. I have to believe in an eternal future with Larry, even a future here with someone else. And that means the church. How can she look at life without the kingdom to live in? I just can't, no matter how it hurts us.

When I took the kids to church later, I knew again I was right. In fact, I wept all through the sacrament. It was just so lovely to be with people and hear the organ music and know that love was all around me and that soon it will take me in again.

The kids scuffled in the back seat on the way home, but somehow I could bear it. I didn't even get near Bishop Ted. I didn't shake his hand to see if mine would burn. It would have. I could feel his eyes on me, even when my vision was wet. I know he understood, that in a way he was holding me.

May 11. The world is beautiful inside and out. Everything has changed. I can see it all now. For the last three days, I've hardly needed sleep or food. I float on a cushion of happiness. I see that the children are beautiful in their health and their high spirits. Even their scabs are only pink now, and I know that someday they'll be gone. Then they'll be completely beautiful again.

I haven't written about it, but I've been wrestling for so long with this caring—oh, call it love for Bishop Ted. It seemed to have no future. Then suddenly I saw that it will work out. I don't know *how* it will work out, but that it *will* work out, like looking back at the present from a distant point. He will work it out. In fact, he is working it out, with his family, with Sally, with the Lord. And before long, he'll understand it all, extend his hand, and call me. And I, already knowing it's right, will come.

This is so beautifully simple. I don't know the answers, but I know there are answers. Before I only saw problems.

I went over to Ellen's and tried to share this with her, how the whole world can come together if there's just enough love. How love is the energy that fuels everything. But she looked at me as if I were really bizarre.

"How much weight have you gained?" she asked.

"I just lost one pound. I don't really need food anymore."

"But before that."

"Oh, maybe thirteen pounds. But it's coming off now. I want to be out in the world walking, maybe even jogging. I want to take my kids to the park. Don't you see? Everything is different."

I could feel myself glowing like she once did. Like bishop Ted. His authority gleams in his dark eyes like the gloss of ripe fruit. His lashes are long and thick.

"Have you been sleeping all right?"

I laughed at her. "Oh, come on, Ellen. You know I was sleeping too much. Now I hardly need sleep at all. I wake up full of energy, thinking how beautiful life is. I remember Larry but without hurting. I see that our life was just—oh, an introduction."

"I think," she said carefully, "that either you're in love or you're a little bit tipsy or a little bit unbalanced."

For a second I was shocked at how the Spirit really does desert people who aren't part of the church anymore. Then I smiled at her and felt light pouring from my face. "Didn't you ever notice how Bishop Ted used to smile at us during the sacrament?" I asked. "The whole congregation. As if he just had his arms around us all? I'm not 'in love,' this is Christ-like love. And it makes the most impossible things possible. It springs the traps."

I have to admit that while picking up the kids at the park (I'd made them promise not to get hurt or talk to strangers), I felt the trap closing a little again. It takes a lot of faith to keep the jaws open. A lot of energy. I know I must keep them open or we will be crushed.

May 12. Only this morning it happened. I woke with his face before me, and I knew. Calmly I fed the children, dressed them, washed their innocent faces, and took them to the park. I handed each a paper sack with the last of our bread and peanut butter in it. How nice it will be to be off food stamps.

On the way to the park, they blew their homemade bubble stuff in the car. Being children, they couldn't wait. Then they slopped some on the seat. I thought of Sally's perfect brood and realized these rascals will have to be introduced one by one. Gradually. As the plan permits.

I wasn't worried. I know he'll have all of this worked out.

I told them to stay on the playground and to be good.

Then I drove here. And now I'm sitting in the car, finishing this entry in front of his house. They haven't noticed me, but I can see them looking like a film of a happy Mormon family cleaning the garage on Saturday morning. Even from here. I can see that Bishop Ted's face is red and sweaty. I can't see his eyes glowing, but I know they do. They will.

As soon as I finish writing, I will take my suitcase from the back seat, shove this journal into the glove compartment, and walk up the driveway. There's a line between the shadow of the garage and the strong, spring sunlight. I will set my suitcase on that line and sit on it, facing him.

When he turns, he'll see me, outlined with light, his vision of what is and what will be. In the bones of my face I can feel how I'll smile when he reaches forth his hand.

WINDOWS ON
THE SEA

STRANGE THAT THE WORLD LOOKED REASSURINGLY the same although Lora Starkham would never look the same to the world. From the stocking-lined mask fitted over her face like a cat burglar, her gray-green eyes observed the traffic around the sunny atrium on the hospital's seventh floor. She was newly grateful for her sight, for the fact that her eyes opened easily. She had been afraid for a time that her eyelids had melted, just as she knew the flesh over her cheekbones and chin had — we are, she observed wryly, clay after all.

Pleasant to sit in the sunlight and crochet with the big hook her seared hands could manage well. She idly watched the medical personnel and the patients in the halls, feeling invisible as only someone who is politely ignored can become. The visitors' occasional second looks at her swathed head no longer stung. She didn't blame them, considering herself the opposite of a blind uncle she had liked, whose emotions played on his face, visible to everyone but him. Besides, she was easily as relieved as the squeamish might be for the mask that postponed the day that her burned, refurbished face must meet air and eyes. Now she was between skin grafts, an ideal oasis, given her condition. The pain was manageable, allowing a private mourning.

Since this was a Sunday, her family would drive the 120 miles from Cedar Springs to Salt Lake City for a visit this afternoon. She would hear Brad's heavy heels crescendo down the hall, although Amy would probably appear first, Luci by the hand. Jake and Marcus would be quarreling without bitterness, ignored by Tim, who was used to it. Luci's red hair would flame like a candle, Lora thought; she envisioned that and the baby's face, bobbing over Brad's shoulder when he turned. She wanted Amber's arms around her neck, a longing tactile as hunger. Missing all of them ached at the core of her pain, yet visiting hours would leave her exhausted, worn by hugs. No kisses these days. No place to kiss.

Now noise of a different sort was approaching and Lora recognized it at once. The teenagers from the disturbed adolescents ward again, fierce in black leather, spiked and colored hair, dripping filthy language, calling each other remarkably hateful names with either venom or affection—hard sometimes to tell. As the clot of them rounded the corner of the atrium, Lora applied herself studiously to her crocheting. They appalled her. Their hostility and boisterousness reminded her why she and Brad had moved their family out of Salt Lake City before Amy began junior high school. Even in Cedar Springs, kids got into trouble, but there was not the drug traffic, the counter-culture, the preponderance of children who seemed to be raising themselves with only their fellow travelers in the streets and alleys for comfort.

"He-ey!" she heard one of them exclaim, as they caught sight of her on the couch, then some laughter before their voices and boot heels faded down the hall. Quiet again.

"I like it," a voice said a minute later, not loudly, but Lora jumped and looked up. One of them, a girl with blue and orange

hair above black-rimmed blue eyes had held back and was loung-
ing, hip out, behind the couch opposite her.

"Excuse me?" Lora said finally.

"I said I like it. Your head gear."

"Oh." Thank you seemed the wrong response. What did
she mean, she liked it? She waited for the girl to go away.

"You think I could get one?"

"Well, I don't know. Why would you want one?"

The girl sighed suddenly, came around the couch and sat
down, thin knees apart in faded jeans. Her black jacket was
slashed down one side and matched her short black boots. Lora
watched her uneasily but she seemed harmless, probably not that
much older than her daughter Amy. For two months before
Lora's accident, Amy had seemed to spend most of her time in
front of the bathroom mirror.

"Seriously," the girl said now. "I would like a mask like
that. Do you think you could get one for me?"

"I have no idea." A pause. "Are you making fun of me?"

The girl leaped up as if she'd been slapped, whirled, then
turned back, her mouth curling downward on one side. "Of
course, I could just do what you did to get one. Burns, right?"

"I don't recommend it. There must be an easier way."

"Good." The girl nodded formally, almost as if curtsying.
"And thanks for not smiling." Turning gracefully in her motorcycle gang garb, she hurried after her peers.

On Monday Lora wept describing her family's visit, which
had gone as usual—too short, too long, the tearing and relief
when they left her there alone. Madeleine, the trauma therapist,
softened her usual piercing gaze and laughed with Lora when
she protested that she couldn't weep properly yet, since her
tear ducts didn't work right. She was beginning to anticipate
going home, sorting like so much laundry what her children's

reactions might be when she wore her strange, new face to PTA meetings, to church, to the park on family outings. The mask first; then the face itself.

"They'd never hate me," she had told Madeleine before losing control, then noticed that Madeleine's eyebrows, always sensitive to nuance, rose.

"What did I say?"

"You said they'd never hate you."

"Oh, hurt me I mean. I meant to say they'd never hurt me."

Madeleine considered. "Hate me is what you said. Maybe you're more deeply concerned than you like to admit."

And that was when she'd started to sob, not at all like the mother she was, but heart-brokenly, as Luci had when her kitten ran into the street.

Lora felt better afterward, all cried out. "Sometimes," she commented, as Madeleine glanced discreetly at the clock on the wall behind her, "I really want to wear this stocking mask forever." That reminded her of the girl in the atrium on Sunday who wanted a mask also, so she told Madeleine about her encounter.

"A thin girl with blue eyes? About five feet tall?"

"Yes. Blue and orange hair."

"The hair changes by the day, sometimes by the hour. She's my client, too. Can you tell me what she said?"

Lora recalled for Madeleine how the girl had pressed her for a mask like her own, developed to apply light pressure to burned tissues and prevent excessive scarring. "A pretty weird request, isn't it."

Madeleine seemed lost in thought. "Maybe." Her hands turned the papers on her desk, then she asked crisply, "Well, do you think you could get one for her?"

"I don't know. Why?"

"Just a hunch. She isn't doing well in therapy, and she's

very troubled. If this is something she wants, maybe it will lead somewhere."

"But if you requested it from the staff," Lora began.

"She asked you," Madeleine said, the piercing look back again. "Maybe you can become a friend. She needs one."

So do I, Lora thought, but not a disturbed alien from another planet, a prospect that weighted her steps back to her room where she fell immediately into a sound sleep.

The next afternoon in the atrium Lora gave Pril—that was her name—the soft stocking worn inside the mask next to the skin. Pril fondled it reverently, but her mouth was snarly. "Did you swipe it?"

"I asked for an extra so I could change it myself if I slopped a little food on it." It had taken far more explanation than that, but Lora didn't elaborate.

Pril nodded. "You didn't say what happened to you."

Lora waved a hand resignedly. "We were up the canyon the week before the Fourth of July. My four-year-old, Luci, came back to where we were toasting marshmallows carrying some fireworks in her hands—Roman candles, giant firecrackers, I've never been sure. Brian and I both yelled at her to stay back, to put them down, but there wasn't time even to slow her down, she was that excited. I felt frozen there by the fire, but I did grab them out of her hands and turned to throw them just as—"

"Pow!" Pril exclaimed.

"Exactly." Lora folded her hands under the pink yarn on her lamp. They hurt and trembled. Pril was silent for perhaps three minutes.

"Sometime," she said shyly, "maybe you could come to my room." Lora was glad the mask hid her surprise and a little annoyance. "I'll perform a meditation for Luci," Pril added, then jumped as a black hand snaked down and flipped a long cigarette butt out of the ash tray. A boy, clad entirely in black except for a red band around his head, smacked his lips at Pril, ignoring Lora. "Hello, Slime-sleaze," Pril said bitterly, as he plopped his other broad hand on her small shoulder. She wound an arm around him and they sauntered toward the elevator, the contraband cigarette entering his back pocket.

"Why Luci?" Lora asked Madeleine later, catching her at the nurse's desk in the burn ward to tell her about Pril's conversation. "Luci didn't get hurt."

"I don't know. Maybe she thinks that Luci assumes blame for your injury, or that you blame Luci."

Lora shook her head. Even in her worst hours, she had been grateful that Luci was not the victim. That would have been infinitely harder to bear. "So strange," Lora mused. "She said maybe I could come to her room and that she would perform a meditation for Luci."

She looked up to find Madeleine staring at her. "She said you could come to her room?" Her tone sounded disbelieving.

"Yes. But should I?"

Madeleine shook her head. "Lora, Pril's room has been off limits to everyone, including the hospital staff. If anyone invades it, she becomes almost catatonic. She has the only private room in that whole ward, possible because there are only three girls now and two of them room together. If she'll allow you to go to her room, by all means go."

Suddenly Lora wanted to go back to her own room and watch something bland and nonsensical on television with her roommate, who had the set on eighteen hours a day. "You make me feel like a spy."

Madeleine took her arm and walked down the hall a few steps. "It's deceptive," she said, "when you see these kids roaming the halls. They've progressed enough to earn that privilege. But they are disturbed, all of them, certainly Pril. How can you be a spy if you help her in ways none of us have been able to so far?"

"Why me?"

"I've considered that," Madeleine said. "Certainly she doesn't warm up to me. Is it because you're so naturally a mother? Or because she sees you as a victim, maybe a fellow victim? Or maybe it is something about your mask. She isn't afraid of what she'll read on your face."

"Does her family visit?"

"We begin family group therapy at our evening session tomorrow night. Pril hasn't been eager to see them. Most of our kids here aren't. War at home, you know." She patted Lora's sleeve and hurried away. "Got a meeting."

Wednesday evening Lora positioned herself outside the small auditorium where a sign announced a family therapy meeting. She took up her crocheting and prepared to scout out Pril's parents. In her bag between the pastel yarns lay Pril's invitation, penned neatly in schoolgirl cursive. "Please come to my room, Windows on the Sea, tomorrow promptly at 2 p.m. My sincere best wishes, Pril." Underneath in very small print between very small parentheses were the numbers 737.

"Why do you call your room, 'Windows on the Sea'?" Lora asked curiously when she read the invitation. "It's very poetic . . . "

"You'll see tomorrow," Pril had said, the words clinging from the corners of her mouth like cigarettes.

What Lora wanted to see first were the parents of these junior gangsters, Pril's in particular. They arrived in ones and twos, the black boy's parents easy to pick out, then the lookalike mother of a blond, heavy girl who always wore a red leather mini. Lora's heart went out to the mother, who looked both respectable and terrified — and very alone. Divorced? Lora wondered. Busy husband? Never married? What could keep a father away from a counseling session when his teenage daughter was hospitalized? Three other couples, one appearing to be a mother and grandfather, entered the auditorium before Lora saw Pril's parents coming and knew at once who they were. The features that on Pril were soft and pixyish — the cherubic mouth, despite its snarl, the upturned nose and eyes — were, on her father, boyish. A cute man, Lora decided; he looked accustomed to loving care and approval, she thought; maybe his mouth seemed a bit spoiled. Pril's mother was a large woman with a dark brown pageboy, apprehensive dark eyes, and a determined chin. Watching her, Lora could feel her worry and had a swift impression that these people were still shocked at the transformation of their sweet, smart daughter.

Pril's parents appeared to be the last couple, and as they approached the auditorium door, the patients filed past Lora and into the auditorium from the opposite direction without a glance to left or right. Lora saw Pril coming at the end of the line and gasped. The whole row of them looked armed for battle, leather, dye, and boots all in place, but Pril had somehow stuffed or shaped the stocking mask she obtained from Lora to resemble a helmet. Then, as Pril smartly turned toward the door, Lora saw where today's paint job had gone. Thick red streamed down the bare backs of her legs, pooling slightly at her shoe tops. Lora's eyes flew to Pril's parents, staring aghast as Pril marched past Lora's line of vision. "Oh my — goodness!" her father breathed, looking to his wife for support; but she was following their daughter, both hands whisking aside tears.

Lora crocheted for some time after the auditorium doors closed, thinking over what she had seen. She felt sick, vulnerable. What children couldn't do to you! Had they no sense of how vulnerable a parent's love is? She imagined the yelling, the stony silence, the defiance or tears, storming behind those doors and had no desire to be in the lobby when the group dispersed. A little shakily, she gathered her yarn and pattern and put them in her bag beside Pril's ladylike invitation. Tomorrow. Weary, she crept back to her room thinking that Amy was already fourteen — and Amy's mother was scarred for life.

During that first visit to Windows on the Sea, Lora was thankful she had brought her bag of handwork with her. She stood outside Room 737 for a few minutes contemplating the ceramic sign below the room number, deciding that Pril had created the graceful nomenclature in a craft class. The sign was pale azure with lettering carefully applied in dark pink, deftly outlined in vermillion. Nervously, Lora lifted her hand and knocked. The door opened.

The room Lora entered was all white — white walls, white ceiling, white tile floor, two white bunks built into the walls. The pillows and sheets were white, and a small, high window caught the pale summer sunlight and threw it back into Lora's eyes. Pril motioned her to sit down on one bunk, then tiptoed to the far corner of the room and performed a pirouette. Lora sat, her eyes on the apparition in front of her. Pril wore no makeup. Her skin was clean and light pink, her brows and lashes barely visible, soft blond like her hair. She wore a light pink leotard, tights, and ballet shoes. Altogether, she was a vision. Lora was speechless, but Pril didn't seem to mind. She hummed as she curled into the corner of the other cot and smiled.

Finally Lora reached into her bag and took out her crocheting, an afghan that was almost finished. "You know," she began, hoping her voice sounded conversational, "you look awfully nice like that."

Pril's eyebrows raised slightly in amusement? scorn? appreciation?

"I've wondered — is Pril short for April?"

Now Pril uncurled like a cat and twirled away from the cot singing (to the tune of "Frere Jacques"), "Princess Prilla, Princess Prilla, Here's your prince. Here's your prince. Prilla is my sweetheart, Prilla is my sweetheart, I'm her prince, I'm her prince."

She ended poised like a doll on a jewelry box. Lora applauded lightly then added, "Oh, Prilla. What a pretty name."

Pril sighed and sat down. A silence followed.

"Pril, what do you do with your time when you're not in therapy or a workshop?"

"Time for you and time for me," Pril said softly, "And time yet for a hundred indecisions, And for a hundred visions and revisions, Before the taking of a toast and tea."

She wandered restlessly for a minute while Lora tried to place that bit of poetry and wondered what it meant to Pril. She had studied it at some point, she knew, but for Pril it seemed precocious.

"Is that Eliot?" she asked finally. Her college poetry class had been a long time back.

Pril smiled, then frowned. "Do I dare disturb the universe? In a minute there is time for decisions and revisions which a minute will reverse."

"I remember that one," Lora said. "At least I think I do. Isn't it Eliot's poem about the cat, the fog? What's the name? The line that's stayed with me is, 'I have measured out my life with coffee spoons.' Except for me, I suppose it would be baby spoons."

Pril was pacing now, a little agitated. "And I have known the eyes already, known them all . . . ," she added, spinning toward Lora accusingly. "The eyes that fix you in a formulated phrase."

The next words popped into Lora's brain and she said them quickly. "And when I am formulated?"

"Sprawling on a pin! When I am pinned and wriggling on the wall, then how should I begin to spit out all the butt ends of my days and ways!"

"Pril," Lora said, rising, "Pril, don't cry." But Pril spun past her to the window and stood staring out.

Lora took up her crochet hook again and waited. As minutes passed, it occurred to her that Pril had not said so much as a sentence of her own. Everything had been verse. After a while she said, "Pril, tell me. Are you upset about the family therapy session last night? I imagine that might be pretty tough."

"I should have been a pair of ragged claws," Pril told the window pane, "scuttling across the floors of silent seas."

"She was like a chrysalis," Lora reported to Madeleine late that afternoon, "pink, newly formed, graceful. She spoke poetry, she danced, she almost cried. She's a beautiful girl, not a hoodlum."

Madeleine listened, clearly impressed. She shook her head. "Poor Pril," she said. "She's like a stone in here—and how did you like her getup last night? You know, now that I think of it, she may have quoted something from that same poem to me once. Which one is it?"

"I looked it up in the big literature book I had Brad bring from home. 'The Lovesong of J. Alfred Prufrock.' "

Madeleine turned to the marker, leafed through the poem and nodded. "Yes, here it is." She looked up, her eyes amused. "Last week when we finished what I thought was an unusually probing conversation—at least I thought we got somewhere— Pril flounced to the door, turned, and said, 'That is not it at all, That is not what I meant, at all.' "

They both laughed. "But what is it?" Lora asked. "I saw her parents. They aren't monsters. What's upsetting her so horribly? She's not crazy?"

A shadow crossed Madeleine's eyes then, and she drew back a little. "She's not responding to therapy. She's protecting someone, maybe her whole family. Her being freaky may be the only way for those she loves to survive, or so it seems to her subconsciously."

"But," Lora began, as Madeleine shook her head and picked up Lora's chart. "So you have skin grafts Monday and then, in a few days, you'll be out of here. We'd better have you ready for that homecoming."

"Yes," Lora said. "I'm trying to get ready."

That night Lora dreamed she was at church with her family. The children were seated all down the pew with Brad at the other end, holding Amber. But no, they weren't all there. Amy was up in front with two other girls her age, who were warbling a hymn. But Amy was belting that song Cindy Lauper had made popular, "Girls Just Wanna Have Fun." Her lank hair had been wound into fancy coils and braids, her glasses hung on a black chain around her neck, her skinny little waist showed between a halter top and shorts that looked so small that even in her dream Lora believed they must be Luci's. Suddenly Lora realized that Luci and the other children were smiling at Amy, cheering her on, to the horror of the other parishioners. "Children!" she whispered, but they turned their faces steadfastly away from her, refused to see, refused to hear. Knowing she was the cause of this uproar, she awoke shivering in her hospital bed.

Lora visited Windows on the Sea again, but this time she did not try so hard to engage Pril in conversation. Lora had a new project, a white quilt top she was edging in blue, this time with a smaller hook—more difficult to wield. Their next-door neighbor's daughter was expecting a baby soon, and Lora wanted to give this former babysitter an unusual and personal gift. Pril seemed at ease, stretching quietly on the other cot, then polishing her nails with clear polish, then simply staring at the ceiling. "I'm going to miss you, Pril," she said finally. "Sometime next week, after my skin graft, I'm going home. Will you write?"

Pril said nothing but stood and stared out the window.

Lora began to gather her things. It would soon be time for dinner and she was hungry. "You'll probably go home before too long," she suggested.

"Pril-la come and dance with me," she heard then and straightened to see Pril curtsy to an imaginary partner. "Both my hands I offer thee." Her hands extended, eyes glazed, Pril was facing but not seeing Lora. Her next gesture was sexual, almost obscene. "Right boob first, left one then; Daddy's girl comes home again."

Pril was still crouched in a bow as Lora, trembling, let herself out the door. Tomorrow, Sunday, she would see her family; the next day, surgery. She walked to the nurse's desk and asked if they would page Madeleine to see if she happened to be anywhere in the hospital. She was.

"Incest!" Lora announced to Madeleine. "That's what it is!"

Madeleine shrugged. "Likely. And she has a younger sister to protect, with two brothers in between."

"I've been sitting here putting things together and I'm furious. You really think that's what it is, why Pril's . . . ?"

"Incest is more common than you think," Madeleine said. "Nobody's admitting it yet, and maybe it's never been fully expressed, but I'm meeting with Pril's parents separately this week."

"But I'm going home next week," Lora said numbly.

"And you have your own problems," Madeleine said. "You have to keep Pril in perspective."

"Thanks, Doc," Lora said and sank back on to the pillows. She doubted she would sleep.

"So, when do you check out," Pril drawled out of the corner of her mouth, dropping down on the sofa opposite Lora who was waiting for her family.

"It depends on how the skin grafts go tomorrow. Will you write to me?"

Pril shrugged and flipped a booted ankle up on one knee. "I'm not much with words."

Lora almost laughed. "I think you do all right."

Pril scowled. "Can you keep your mask?"

"For a while. I don't know how much longer."

Pril blew upward at the bangs on her forehead and sighed. "So I guess you just can't wait to get home, right?"

"Yes and no. In some ways it will be hard."

The scowl stayed, but Pril began nodding slightly. "Yeah. Me too. Like, I know my dad needs me."

"Mmmm," Lora agreed carefully. "And your mom?"

"My mother was always fighting for me," Pril growled, getting up abruptly.

"Good for her."

Pril wheeled. "What? You fight with your kids?"

Lora took a deep breath and tried to sound as level as Madeleine would. "That's not what you said, Pril. You said, 'My mother was always fighting *for* me.' And I saw your mother. I think that's probably true."

Pril arched like an offended cat. "So screw you, Lora. Mothers always stick together, right?" She flounced away.

Lora's family came and went, then the anesthesiologist, the surgeon, Madeleine and, in the morning, all of them again. Time drifted, and she with it, in and out of mists and dreams, familiar now from the weeks after her accident and the surgeries that followed. Once or twice she thought Pril floated through the mist, but words were bright kites with hairlike strings; she could seldom catch one and pull it in before it blew past her.

Wednesday came sharp and clear. Lora showered, ate, talked with the surgeon and Madeleine, walked twice through the halls, then returned and reached for her tote bag. She sorted through it twice before she realized that the white quilt top, now halfway edged with blue, simply wasn't there.

Of course, she knew at once where it had gone. She hurried down the hall toward the disturbed adolescent ward, anger quickening her steps. The anger felt good, a righteous indignation toward all the wrongs of children toward parents, the careless pranks and thoughtless acts that betrayed in an instant years of devotion. Rounding the corner she paused at the drinking fountain, fingers shielding the edges of her mask. She reminded herself as she drank the icy water until her teeth ached that she should not, could not, let what might be her parting incident with Pril be a sour one. She must find some way to let her know that stealing her work was unacceptable but that she was still accepted. Maybe, she thought, her anger lightening, she could find out why Pril did it.

She stood outside the door, admired the ceramic sign again, then tapped lightly.

"Pril, it's Lora."

Cautiously, Lora opened the door slightly, then more. She could see Pril's bare leg and foot prone and pale on her cot. Her heart leaped, and she shoved the door open wide, bursting into the room in one motion. But Pril was only asleep, sound asleep, and nude. Draped across her, one corner tucked under her chin, the other in her crotch like a diaper, was Lora's quilt-top, except that now it was lurid with color, defaced as Pril often defaced her body, her hair.

Why? Lora wondered, outraged on behalf of the blue cro-cheted edging that had been so difficult to accomplish with the small hook and her injured hands. "Pril!" She stepped closer.

Pril was breathing as steadily as a baby. Close up, Lora could see words on the fabric, colored in Pril's neat cursive. Tip-ping her head, she could read a few. "Always Fighting For Me." So she had taken that sentence Lora had challenged with her back to her room. This sentence didn't rhyme or chime except — maybe — with truth. Beneath it Pril slept like a soldier wrapped in her flag. Markers littered the foot of the bed.

Lora looked up and away as her eyes burned with the tears that still couldn't quite flow. Outside Pril's small window, the sky was a flaming glory, and Lora stood on her toes, knees pressed against the cot for a better look. Purple and gold streaks soared above an improbable peach glow at the horizon. As she watched, the lower rims of the high mauve clouds singed like brimstone, then billow after billow caught and flared. Minutes passed before she realized that the igniting rays flashed upward from the salty lake, a thin, silver streak she hadn't noticed before at this distance. Pril's slight snoring underscored Lora's breaths that drew in color and light, spilling all her eyes couldn't absorb like a blessing on the girl beside her. What if I had lost my sight, she thought, and missed this?

How many evenings, she wondered, had Pril knelt on her bed to watch this long embrace of sun and lake? Often enough to name her room Windows on the Sea; frequently enough to sanctify this cell that beamed scarlet from its vacant walls to poetry and motion. Enough to let the girl within the scaly armor emerge and shine.

Lora considered the quilt-top again. Finally she selected a blue marker from the foot of the bed. She stooped beside the free corner of the quilt. "For Pril," she printed neatly, "with love, because we're both finding our way home."

ACKNOWLEDGEMENTS

"The Last Day of Spring" first appeared in *Dialogue: A Journal of Mormon Thought* 14 (Winter 1981), 4.

"Susanna in the Meadow" first appeared in *Utah Holiday,* Aug. 1986.

"The Spiral Stair" first appeared in *Sunstone* 11 (July 1987), 4.

"Second Tuesday: Lunch" first appeared in *Network*, Aug. 1986.

"Mornings" first appeared in *Dialogue: A Journal of Mormon Thought* 19 (Spring 1986), 1.

"Bishop Ted" first appeared in *Sunstone* 10 (Feb. 1985), 2.

"A String of Intersections," "Payday," "Coyote Tracks," "He Called Us Mormon Nuns," and "Windows on the Sea" appear here for the first time.